WORTHY OF LOVE

NEW YORK TIMES BESTSELLING AUTHOR

Carly Phillips

Can One night of passion make him feel worthy of love?

Police officer Kevin Manning feels responsible for his partner's death. Nikki Welles is grieving the loss of her brother, the only family she had left.

One night of shared passion leads to so much more than either anticipated—

A baby he'd never expected.

Another opportunity to get things right.

If only he can convince her to give him a second chance.

"Hot heroes, serious passion and characters with emotional depth."
—Bella Andre, NY Times Bestselling Author

* * *

PROLOGUE

*H*e killed his partner. He might as well have taken the gun and pulled the trigger himself. Only forty-eight hours had passed during which he'd doubted anything would help him forget. How ironic it was that the woman in his bed had done what a bottle of scotch could not. She'd been a blessing, something he didn't deserve.

She tossed and turned in her sleep. He understood the source of her distress; it was his as well. Grief washed over her in waves, burrowing into her heart, reaching deep inside her soul. He knew and felt her pain as if it were his own. He should, considering he was the cause. Yet she'd reached out for him and he hadn't been able to turn her away. Not when she'd looked to him for comfort, and not, damn him, when comfort had turned to desire.

He dressed in silence, not wanting to wake her, not wanting to face what he'd done. He'd slept with Nicole. Worse, he'd never felt so close so fast, never felt anything so right. He exhaled a harsh groan but she didn't stir.

When he screwed up, he screwed up royally. He'd arrived on the scene too late to help, but in time to watch his partner die. He'd been too busy tending to his drunken father and Tony was dead because of it.

Then, when Tony's sister had turned up on his doorstep seeking comfort, he had taken her to bed. If he were capable of real emotion, he'd think they had more than just sex. He knew better. Guilt weighed heavily because Tony was dead and he wasn't. Because he'd let his partner down. Twice. Because Nikki, for all her bravado last night, was an innocent. He muttered a curse and allowed himself one last glance at the rumpled bed. Her black hair stood out in stark contrast against the white sheets and her soft skin beckoned to him. He wanted nothing more than to join her, to lose himself in her once more, because she'd brought him more peace than he'd ever known. More than he deserved. If he thought he could bring anything good to her life… He shook his head in disgust.

He knew what he was, who he was. Hadn't the events of the past two days proven he wasn't any good at caring for anyone but himself? He tossed his duffel bag over his shoulder and did what he did best: He turned and walked out the door without looking back.

ONE

Kevin Manning let himself into the rambling house he'd inherited a month ago. No sound greeted him as he entered, just the echo of his shoes on the hardwood floor. The quiet enveloped him, welcomed him home and left him alone with his thoughts. Not a pleasant place to be lately. Maybe he ought to get a dog. At least someone would get some use out of the grassy backyard. And he could use the company.

He tossed his keys onto the kitchen counter and grabbed a cold bottle of beer from the fridge. He picked up his house phone receiver and heard the annoying sound that alerted him that he had messages. He dialed his code and the digital voice announced one message. He tilted the bottle to his lips and let a hefty sip of brew slide down his throat as the first call played.

"Hey, sonny boy. My birthday and you couldn't be bothered to lift the goddamned phone." A gritty, drunken chuckle followed. "If it weren't for me, you wouldn't even be on this planet so give the old man a call. Better yet, stop by. I'm dying of thirst."

The smooth taste turned sour in his mouth and he headed for the kitchen to pour the nearly full bottle down the drain. The old man might claim all Mannings were alike and Kevin might have proven him right only two short months ago, but he'd be damned if he'd willingly take another step toward hell.

On the way home, he'd stopped by the seedy apartment where he'd grown up, drawn in by the continuing sense of obligation he lived with on a daily basis. Peering through the window, he'd seen his father passed out on the couch, bottle of scotch in hand. Visiting would have been useless and Kevin had given up trying to reform him years ago. He'd only gotten smacked around for his trouble. Instead, he kept tabs on the old man and made sure he had a roof over his head – not that his father appreciated the gesture.

A persistent ring brought him out of the past and he glanced at the caller id on the receiver. Whether the voicemail picked up the call or he did, Kevin would have to deal with his so-called father. Might as well get it over with.

An hour later, he walked toward a nearby bar, wishing he'd let the voicemail screen his calls. Even dealing with the old man would be preferable to this. He'd only been back in town for a couple of weeks, and he'd planned on dealing with his recent past, but on his own terms – when he was ready to face the casualties his actions had caused.

Kevin pulled open the door with the word STARS etched into the fogged glass. He had no business being in a place like this, but he hadn't chosen the location any more than he'd wanted the meeting. He entered the upscale establishment and grabbed a seat by the bar. A club with fancy theme drinks and wall-to-wall suits wasn't the place he'd pick to spend his down time, but he had to admit that it beat the empty place he now called home.

He ordered a club soda from the bartender, kicked back, and took in his surroundings. From his cushioned stool, he had a perfect view of the front door and, thanks to the mirrored walls around him, a sweeping angle of the back twenty tables which had yet to be filled. A seductive-looking waitress with dark hair and a bottle of cleaning fluid made her way between the tables, pausing only to spray and wipe before moving on to the next target.

Kevin watched her, appreciating the soft sway of her hips as she moved to the beat of the music. She leaned over the glass tabletops, giving him an enticing view of a firm ass enclosed in tight denim and long legs covered by black cowboy boots. As she headed for the next table, she paused, glancing back toward the bar and its growing number of customers before swinging around once more. Kevin choked on a gulp of club soda.

In the brief second during which he caught a glimpse of her face, the sexy waitress had reminded him of Nikki. He hadn't thought of her in a while, hadn't allowed himself the pain... or the pleasure – except in his dreams, where control deserted him and desire took over. In his more rational waking moments, he knew the night couldn't have been as good as he remembered; and, even if it was, two months had passed, enough time to put the thought of her behind him. And he had. He wouldn't be thinking of her now if Tony's widow hadn't called and asked to meet him.

Kevin focused on the waitress as she polished the brass railings above the booths. Small waist, just narrow enough for his fingers to span, and impossibly long legs. He shifted uncomfortably in his seat. Yeah, she resembled Nikki all right. He and Tony had been partners for eight years and, during that time, he'd come to know Nikki pretty well. Funny how he hadn't thought of her as anything other than Tony's kid sister, not until their last night together, when he'd learned she was more than he'd ever dreamed.

All the facts he knew about Nicole told him he wouldn't find Tony's sister working in a place like this. Last time he'd seen her she'd been one semester short of her teaching degree, not drink-serving 101.

He glanced at her doppelgänger. If his eyes had to play tricks on him, at least he had a hell of a view. He downed the last of his soda and gestured for another, never taking his eyes from the long legs that sparked his memory. Of him helping Nikki lift her flowing skirt around her waist, of pushing aside the soft fabric and burying himself inside her warmth. Nikki had wrapped those legs around his waist many times that night. She might have been innocent when they started, but not when dawn finally broke and the night came to an end. She'd been eager, willing and he hadn't thought to stop. He hadn't thought beyond the driving need to block out the numbing grief and guilt over his role in his partner's death.

For a few hours, she'd done the impossible. She'd allowed him to forget. Even now his body reacted to the thought of Nikki as if she were standing before him. As if time, circumstance, and his fatal error in judgment had never happened. But it had. Meeting Tony's widow in this bar was proof of that. *What did Janine need to talk about?* he wondered.

He heard his name and realized he'd have his answer soon enough. He tore his gaze away from the dark-haired waitress. A last glance at the seductress in the form-fitting top and tight jeans negated any lingering doubts. Tony's hearth-and-home sister wouldn't be serving drinks in a downtown bar.

Kevin led Janine to an empty table in the rear. The waitress had disappeared. He kicked back in his seat. He'd stay long enough to hear what she had to say. He'd make sure she was okay and then he'd be on his way. "So…"

"Can I get you folks a drink?"

Kevin couldn't mistake the husky voice tinged with a trace of midwestern twang and he jerked his head up in response. He raised his gaze to find himself staring into stunned but familiar violet eyes. Eyes that had seen inside his soul, only this time they were outlined in a smoky color that added to her allure. So he hadn't imagined the resemblance, but that's all there was.

The cocktail waitress standing before him in the black spandex V-neck top that exposed more than a generous hint of cleavage wasn't the Nikki he remembered. Her dramatically made-up face wasn't the only change, but he had to admire the new version.

If the fresh-faced girl from the Midwest had the ability to knock a jaded cop off his feet, what would this sexy siren do if given the chance? He had no desire to find out. But he would indulge his curiosity. Nikki had changed too much in too short a period of time and makeup wasn't the only visible difference. A weariness etched her delicate features and grief still haunted her eyes. Her emotions were visible for all to see and damned if it didn't make him want her more. It also made him furious that life could hurt and change her so drastically.

Reminding himself he was a part of that hurt, he decided to tread carefully. He leaned back in his seat, resting an elbow on the cushioned armrest. "Nikki."

Her eyes had widened in surprise but to her credit, she regained her composure quickly. "Kevin," she murmured, as softly and as seductively as if she'd just seen him last night and not two long months ago. If not for the way her fingers clutched her round tray, turning her knuckles white, he'd have thought her completely unaffected.

"Beer, right?" she asked.

"Club soda."

She raised an eyebrow. He didn't explain but he wasn't surprised she remembered his preference. Though she'd lived on campus, she'd spent weekends with Tony and Janine. When not on duty, Kevin had spent holidays and football season Sundays in their home. The reminder of Tony only sharpened the ever-present pain in his chest.

Nikki turned her now-furious gaze to Janine. "Since it's Patriot's Day here in Boston, maybe you'd like one of tonight's specials. A Benedict Arnold seems just your speed. If it's not on the menu, I'm sure the bartender would do me a favor and create one just for you." She treated her sister-in-law to a forced smile. "On the house."

"Make it a ginger ale," Janine said without reacting to Nikki's dig.

"I'll be back with your drinks." Nikki turned and walked away.

Kevin forced his gaze off Nikki and the men at the bar who ogled her as she passed. Checking his emotions was difficult, but he pushed his feelings aside before turning back to Janine.

"You ambushed me." He darted a glance over his shoulder. "And I don't think she was expecting this visit either." If he hadn't thought of Nikki as being hours away, busy finishing school and earning her degree, he'd have realized she was the source of Janine's call. She was the sexy waitress and he had been set up.

Janine shrugged, a satisfied smile on her face. "I had no choice."

"We all have choices, Janine."

"Exactly." She folded her arms on the table and leaned forward. "You made yours that night in your apartment."

If he had any doubts about what Janine knew—or
didn't know—about his relationship with Nikki, she'd
just put them to rest. He didn't begrudge Nikki a
shoulder to lean on, but he felt as if Tony were here,
condemning him through his wife.

"Now, aren't you in the least bit curious about
hers?"

"Should I be?"

She shook her head. "You tell me. The night of the
shooting, I remember you telling me that Tony asked
you to look out for his family before he died."

His stomach churned at the reminder of the night
he couldn't put to rest. "He asked that I make sure his
family… you and Nikki… were okay. I did that."

"By taking off? By not checking in, not once for
the last two months?"

"You wouldn't have wanted to hear from me."

"Not true. Nobody blames you, Kevin. *I* don't
blame you."

He slammed his hand down on the table. "*I* blame
me." If he hadn't been babysitting his father, Max,
Tony wouldn't have run off alone when he'd gotten
the call to head over to a domestic dispute. Tony
wouldn't be dead and he wouldn't be sitting here with
his partner's widow.

"So that's how you handle guilt? That's how you

keep a promise?"

"By quitting the force and letting you two get on with your lives," he explained. "Without any painful reminders."

Janine's laughter took him by surprise. "Is that what you think you did?" She sobered suddenly and studied his face. "Life went on, Kevin. But not the way you think."

"Meaning?"

Janine's arm swept the expanse of the bar, to where Nikki maneuvered between customers, taking orders and serving drinks. "Need I say more?" Janine asked.

"What happened to her degree? She only had one semester left of student teaching."

"You want information, I suggest you ask her yourself."

He paused then, realizing for the first time that he had no idea how Nikki or Janine had gotten on since Tony's death. Janine had Tony's pension, but was it enough?

And where did that leave Nikki? Her parents' savings at the time of their death had been minimal. The farm had been mortgaged twice and he remembered Tony telling him the creditors had taken nearly everything, including insurance from the fire. *With her brother, her only family and source of support gone, what choices had Nikki been forced to make?* Kevin wondered. For a change, he hadn't thought of anyone, taken care of anyone, but himself.

His old man's favorite words came back to haunt him. *Mannings were no good at taking care of anyone but themselves.* His dead partner had been his first wake-up call, Nikki his second.

His gaze wandered to the woman he couldn't forget. She stood, leaning over a male customer. The surge of jealousy was so strong and so foreign to him, Kevin barely heard Janine as she spoke. "She needs you."

Nikki laughed at something the guy said and his hand cupped her waist in an all too-familiar grip. She didn't seem inclined to walk away. Kevin forced his gaze off Nikki's waist and back to Janine. "Seems to me like she's doing just fine on her own," he said.

Janine shot him a disbelieving stare. "I doubt Tony would agree."

"Cheap shot," he muttered.

"But true." As she spoke, Nikki returned.

Despite the smoke, despite the distinct odor of alcohol, Kevin was aware of her. Her unique scent had lingered in his dreams and as she circled their seats, pausing only to slam down their drinks before moving on, he could swear she still wore the same perfume.

He watched her in action. She served neighboring

tables, pausing to talk at some, flirt at others, and avoid wandering hands as she worked. From the easy way she maneuvered, he'd guess she'd been doing this for more than just a few nights. He looked to Janine for answers, but after having set him up, his companion disappeared.

He exhaled a groan. Nikki had a new look, a new job. From all outward appearances, she had a whole new life. One he was damn sure her brother wouldn't approve of, one that put Kevin in a position he didn't want to be in.

He'd left the morning after, believing that Nikki would be better off going on with her life without him around. After all, if his partner couldn't count on him, what could he offer Nikki? She deserved better than him. He glanced around the crowded bar. Better than this, too. Kevin knew all about these places firsthand. He'd grown up hanging around the sleazier bars, tagging after his drunken father.

Knowing Nikki was subjecting herself to the leers and come-ons he'd seen his father make… Even if the guys wore suits instead of an out-of-work plumber's overalls, they were after the same thing. From Nikki. The thought made him sick and Kevin refused to dwell on it any longer. Instead he settled in.

Throughout the night, Nikki glared at him plenty and refilled his drink once, but she didn't stop to talk.

Obviously, she planned to ignore him until he decided to leave. With his track record, she probably figured it was only a matter of time. He wished he could oblige. Watching Nikki had aroused more than his curiosity and he didn't like the feeling. He'd prefer to put it, and her, behind him as soon as possible.

And he would, as soon as he fulfilled his promise to Tony. Last time he left, he did so based on the assumption that Nikki would be fine without him. He'd been so wrapped up in himself and his mistakes that he'd made another one.

He'd left without checking facts, a damn stupid move for an ex-cop. Before he dropped out of sight again, he intended to make sure he accomplished his goal.

* * *

Nikki Welles grabbed her fake fur coat from the hook in the back hall and glanced around the empty bar once more. Not a customer or ex-lover in sight. Apparently, things hadn't changed. He still made his getaway before facing her one-on-one. She fought back the recurring wave of nausea that threatened to overtake her. She'd been queasy before work and hadn't been able to eat and once here, greasy bar food didn't appeal to her weak stomach.

Ever since her brother's death, she was lightheaded

and woozy most of the time. Similar to when her parents had died, but much, much worse. She and Tony had been very close... and now she had no one but Janine. At one time, she thought she'd have Kevin, but he hadn't cared enough to stick around, and obviously that hadn't changed.

His generous tip didn't ease the insult; it merely heightened it, especially since she hadn't earned the money. He'd taken up space at her station and paid her for nothing. As if he felt sorry for her. The thought brought back painful memories she believed she'd put behind her... of the morning she'd woken up in his apartment, alone in his bed.

At first she'd thought he was somewhere around. Then, not wanting to believe the worst, she convinced herself he'd gone down to pick up breakfast for them both. She'd even set the table, pulled on the shirt he'd left near the bed and curled up to wait. Only after an embarrassing amount of time had passed, did she accept the truth. He considered her a mistake and he'd left her in his apartment rather than face her the morning after, probably giving her time to gather her things and leave before he returned. Just the memory brought back the rush of shame she'd felt at the time, but only for a moment. Because Kevin Manning wasn't worth it... even if he still looked sexy enough to knock her off her feet. She'd never go there again.

She wrapped her coat around her body and headed for the door. "Sure you don't want to wait five?" one of the bartenders asked as she passed.

"No, thanks. I'll be fine." She waved good night and ducked into the cool night air before he could argue. The taxi routinely picked her up on the corner of the one-way street. Most nights, one of the guys kept her company on her walk, but tonight, she wanted to be alone. She needed to think about what Kevin's return meant for her future and what form of revenge would work best on the sister-in-law who had betrayed her.

She exhaled, watching the puff of air hover and disappear. With the chill in the air, she found it hard to believe spring was on the way. She bowed her head down and walked to the corner, her hand wrapped around the pepper spray she kept in her coat pocket as a precaution. The streets were quiet, but the guys at work had taught her never to take safety for granted. From the beginning, they'd looked at her as their naïve kid sister, which, for the most part, she had been. They'd taught her how to flirt when appropriate, duck a come-on when necessary, and how to take care of herself.

As she reached the corner, someone grabbed her arm and she swung around, pepper spray in her other hand. As quickly as she'd turned, she found herself disarmed and pulled against a lean, hard body, her face pressed against cold leather. Heart pounding, throat dry, she grappled for a way out and remembered the night's tips tucked safely inside her boots. She wondered if her attacker would be satisfied with that or if he wanted something more. Something she wouldn't willingly give.

Before she could process that thought, he released her. She stumbled backward and looked up to see Kevin, pepper spray in hand and a dark scowl on his face.

She drew in a ragged breath. The cold air did nothing to calm her nerves or her shaking hands. Even as she glared at him, she couldn't help the awareness that shot through her veins. He hadn't changed. He oozed sex appeal and raw danger. With his dark hair, razor stubble and black leather jacket, he was a part of the streets and the black night that stretched out before them. He was a loner, belonging on his own, much more than he'd ever belong to anyone else. She'd been foolish to hope he'd ever be hers.

"I didn't believe those rumors until I saw you in the bar," she said when she'd caught her breath. "You have resurfaced."

TWO

K evin didn't smile. In fact, his eyes darkened until they matched the color of the night sky. "And you don't look too pleased that I have."

"What do you expect? You scared me half to death. What's wrong with you, sneaking up on me like that?" Nikki rubbed her arm where he'd grabbed her, more from a sense of shock than anything else. He hadn't hurt her, not physically anyway.

"Join the club, princess. Just watching you tonight scared the hell out of me."

Her heart skipped a beat at the endearment he so casually tossed her way. He'd always called her princess, from the first moment they'd met. He'd called her princess that night, too, when he'd thrust inside her and realized she was a virgin. She should have told him, but she'd been too afraid he'd turn her away if she had. The risk was too great. She'd needed the comfort as much as she'd needed *him*.

He'd kissed away her tears and reached past her childish fantasies to what she'd foolishly believed was reality. In so doing, he'd touched her heart... and trampled on it the following day. Never again, she reminded herself and breathed deeply, allowing the cold air to clear her mind. Even the nausea seemed to fade, courtesy of the fresh air.

"What's wrong with *you*?" he asked.

"Excuse me?" She blinked at his harsh tone of voice.

"What have you done with your life? Giving up teaching to work in a place like that." He gestured toward the bar down the street. "Letting strange men paw you," he continued without missing a beat. "Walking the streets alone in the dead of night, dressing like a... like a..." He shook his head and trailed off, obviously losing steam.

"Don't stop now," she murmured. "Not when you're just getting interesting. Dressing like a... what?" she prompted.

"Forget it. Just tell me what the hell's going on."

"I don't know what you mean." She blinked twice, feigning ignorance, buying time. Student teachers didn't earn money and she'd been forced to give up her scholarship because she couldn't afford housing on campus or otherwise. Her life had changed so fast, she could hardly believe it herself.

Explaining would take more energy than she possessed and she refused to bare her soul to a man who didn't care. "And even if I did, I wouldn't tell you," she said, turning the brunt of her true feelings on him. There was a time when she'd have told him anything, but not anymore. She spun on her heels, intending to walk away.

He stopped her with a hand on her shoulder. No force, no strength to his grip, just a touch... and she turned back toward him. "Tony wouldn't approve," he said softly.

"Tony's not here," she reminded him, forcing the words past the catch in her throat. He muttered a harsh curse. She glanced up, hating the tears in her eyes, hating that he'd see her weakness. When she was weak she was at her most vulnerable, and she'd worked too hard to be strong.

"But I am." He touched her cheek with one hand, with a single stroke of his calloused finger. The warmth shot straight through her, settling in her chest, perilously close to her heart.

Nikki fought the feeling and let his words register instead. Then she looked at him and laughed. She couldn't help it, couldn't control her reaction to what he'd just said because she'd come to him once before. She'd leaned on him, opened her heart, and relied on him to be there for her afterward. He hadn't been. Instead he'd taken off and left her alone.

As if she'd slapped him, he jerked his hand away from her face. The cold wind blew across her cheek and the chill went much deeper than her skin. She wrapped her arms around herself, but she didn't feel warmer. Being alone, hurt, she admitted to herself, but better being alone than rejected again. No matter how much she needed someone, she wouldn't turn to Kevin. She didn't trust him to be there when she fell.

"I don't need you," she told him. The nausea she'd suffered from earlier returned in force, but she fought against the wave that assaulted her. A few more minutes and she'd be on her own, and she could collapse in private. "Tony would have respected any well-thought-out decision and I've made mine. You'll have to accept it even if you don't understand."

He muttered something that sounded suspiciously like "We'll see about that."

"It isn't your place to see or not." She took two steps and her knees buckled.

Kevin saved her from falling by wrapping an arm around her waist and pulling her close. "Apparently, it is. You're overworked, exhausted and…"

"Just a little nauseous, dizzy. I'm fine or I will be after a good night's sleep."

His eyes narrowed as his dark gaze focused in on

her. "Has this happened before?"

"Yes. No." She could barely think, let alone answer. Maybe if his strength weren't so potent, his scent so seductive, she wouldn't feel as dizzy and overwhelmed.

All her energy went into remaining upright and focused. Once she got rid of Kevin, she could collapse in a taxi and pull herself together.

"Well, which is it?" he asked.

Nikki shook her head, but the rapid movement only made things worse. The last thing she felt before blackness claimed her was his strong arms beneath her knees and his softly muttered curse in her ear.

*　*　*

The sound of oil splattering in a frying pan woke her. It wasn't the first time Nikki had opened her eyes since falling into the uncharacteristic faint.

She'd awakened earlier to find herself in Kevin's car, his hand stroking her cheek as he drove. Because she'd been so exhausted, she hadn't fought him. Lulled by the motion of the vehicle and the illusion of security she'd desperately needed, she'd allowed herself to drift back to sleep.

She swung her legs over the side of what she now realized was an unfamiliar couch and sat up. Her stomach rebelled at the sudden upward movement.

Breathe deep. Nikki obeyed her silent command, but the odor of frying eggs worked against her.

"Bathroom's over there."

Nikki heard him and ran, making it just in time. How an empty stomach could cause so much trouble, she had no idea. When the shaking stopped and she felt steady enough to rise, she splashed cold water on her face and prepared to approach Kevin.

"You okay?"

She glanced up to find him standing in the doorway, his brow furrowed in concern, "Yeah." She pushed her hair out of her eyes, barely able to meet his gaze. Throwing up wasn't an everyday occurrence. Having an audience, especially having Kevin as an audience, made the situation even worse.

"Here, let me help you to the table." He took a step toward her, but embarrassment forced her retreat. The back of her legs hit the toilet and he laughed. "I think I've already witnessed your worst," he said. "Shutting me out now won't make things better. Let me help." His voice dropped an octave as he held out a hand.

She nodded and placed her palm inside his. Heat shot through her arm, setting off a warm tingling in her chest and stomach – one which she'd prefer to attribute to dizziness and exhaustion, *not* to Kevin's potent touch.

She glanced at her watch. Only an hour since she'd left the bar. "Why didn't you just take me home?" she asked.

"I figured you needed someone to keep an eye on you and Janine needs her sleep."

"So you volunteered for the job?"

"I didn't see anyone else around to catch you when you fell."

"Thank you for that," she murmured, realizing that she sounded like an ungrateful bitch.

"You're welcome." He pulled an old wooden chair from beneath the bleached oak table. The set was obviously piecemeal, an old rectangular table, two matching chairs and an odd assortment of others.

"Yours?" she asked, remembering a plain white table in his old apartment.

He followed her line of vision. "Came with the house," he explained.

"House." Nikki lowered herself into the chair before she had another wave of dizziness to contend with. "I thought you rented an apartment?" She kept her gaze glued to the scarred table, refusing to let the memories of *that* night, *that* place, resurface.

"It was a month-to-month lease, furniture and all. The morning I left..." He cleared his throat, obviously as uncomfortable with the memories as she. "When I left, I dropped a check with the landlord for an extra month's rent along with a note asking him to store my things."

He'd given the landlord more consideration than he'd given her, she thought. "And this house?"

"Was left to me by an aunt who remembered me in her will. I figured it was as good an excuse as any to come back to town."

"It was, but I wasn't." Nikki could have bitten her tongue in two the minute the words were out of her mouth. She knew, without question, what that night had meant to him. What she meant to him. Nothing. Not a damn thing. He'd used her to forget the pain, the same pain she'd been reeling from. Only difference was, she'd been drawn to him for months, probably years, and being in his arms had been an answer to all her dreams. Or so she'd thought.

He poured a can of cola into a glass and put it down in front of her. "Drink this. The sugar will help the dizziness and since I rarely touch the stuff, it's probably flat and will settle your stomach."

"How would you know?"

"My old man suffered from enough hangovers in his time."

She wrapped her hands around the cold glass. "I wasn't drunk."

"Upset stomach. Close enough, now drink. Then we'll talk."

Her eyelashes fluttered down and she complied with his command. Almost immediately, the rolling in her stomach had begun to ease.

"Better?" he asked.

She nodded.

"Now, has this happened before?"

"Not like this. I work nights and with the stress of the last couple of months... I'm just tired." Her stomach chose that moment to remind them both that she hadn't eaten all day.

He grinned at the loud rumbling that echoed in the kitchen.

"And hungry," she admitted.

"I already dumped the eggs."

"I couldn't get those down anyway." She doubted much of anything would sit well in her stomach, except... "Do you have any ice cream?" she asked hopefully, licking her lips at the thought of the cold treat easing its way down her parched throat.

"Yes."

"And french fries?"

"You're kidding."

She shook her head. "Now that I've gotten my appetite back, I have this urge for french fries, too. Any in the freezer?"

He raised an eyebrow at her unusual request. "Sorry, but no."

"Then it's a good thing there's an all-night fast food place near my apartment." She graced him with a smile. "We can stop by... on my way home," she said pointedly.

"You obviously can't wait to get away from me. Fine, but from the looks of things, you've been neglecting your health, and that's got to stop."

She glanced down at her too-thin body. Being overworked and exhausted had taken their toll. She shouldn't care that he looked and found her lacking, but vanity won out. She more than cared... and didn't appreciate the silent admission. "Thanks for the compliment," she said wryly. "And here I thought I've never looked better."

His eyes fell to her chest, then traced a heated path over the rest of her body and up again. Her breasts tightened and swelled beneath his visual caress. "Why are you looking at me like that?" she asked, uncomfortable under his scrutiny.

"Ice cream and french fries isn't exactly a typical combination."

She shrugged. "Works for me. Can we go?"

"In a minute."

"I don't have a minute. It's almost four in the morning and I have to work tomorrow night. That means I need a decent meal and sleep... not necessarily in that order."

He braced his hands on his thighs and rose from his seat, crossing until he stood before her. His strong hand reached out and touched her cheek. The pad of his thumb stroked beneath her eye. "Looks to me like you haven't been getting much of either. Sleep or food. But I'll go along for now. French fries it is."

She followed him toward the garage, her gaze taking in his broad shoulders, the narrowed waist and the way his denim jeans hugged his ass. Memories and need assailed her.

She didn't want this pull toward him complicating the life she was just beginning to build. "And then we'll go home?" she asked.

His gaze settled on hers, intense and serious. "Yes, Nikki. And then *we'll* go home."

* * *

Kevin watched as Nikki inhaled fries and a burger, as if she hadn't eaten in ages. He would have found the sight amusing, if he wasn't so concerned.

"French fry?" she asked, holding the bag out toward him.

"No thanks."

She shrugged. "That's okay. More for me."

He didn't know whether to tell her not to overdo it or to let her make up for lost time. Before he could decide, she distracted him with a question.

"Tell me where you've been all this time," she said in between bites.

"The Florida Keys."

Her eyes grew wide, but the pain there was obvious. "I'm glad you were soaking up the sunshine."

He had no difficulty reading her mind or the betrayal she obviously felt. "While you and Janine were grieving, you mean."

She glanced down. "Whatever."

Reaching out, he lifted her chin with his hand. "It's not whatever, it's important. The truth always is and I wasn't out enjoying the sunshine, I was making myself scarce so you two could heal." He drew a deep, painful breath. "And I was grieving myself."

He wondered if she'd go that one step further and ask why he'd walked out on her, but she jerked her head out of his grasp. "Makes for a good story," she muttered.

Realizing he'd been given a reprieve, he glanced down. A few more fries remained. "Eat up."

"I'm not hungry anymore. I'd like to go home."

"I'm always happy to oblige."

The sun was just peeking over the horizon as Nikki entered Janine's apartment building with Kevin following close behind. She walked down the long hallway leading to the apartment. The lingering odors of food and the musty scent that always permeated the air seemed stronger now. Her full stomach didn't appreciate the mixture of smells and she swallowed a groan.

"Do you have your key?" Kevin asked.

"Of course." She wanted to get away from him as soon as possible.

He'd sat across from her in the tight booth, and with little room beneath the table, his legs entwined with hers. Her body *still* vibrated from his heat and the strength of his muscles pressing against her. She fished through her pocket and withdrew the key her brother had given her long ago, then turned to place it in the lock. As soon as she got to the other side of that door, she'd be free of this insane pull that Kevin still had over her. Free of him. Unfortunately, Kevin had other ideas.

He plucked the key from her hand, taking control. She withheld a protest, knowing it would do no good, and waited for him to let her inside. Instead, he turned toward her. Leaning back against the old chipped paint, his massive shoulders surrounded by the doorframe, he loomed large before her.

Wall sconces provided the only source of light in the otherwise darkened hall. Not all of them worked, but the nearest one provided a backdrop for Kevin. The light shone on his raven-colored hair and illuminated his recently acquired tan, his skin, sun-kissed in the Florida Keys. Despite what she'd intimated, she believed that he was grieving, too. She just had a hard time accepting his sudden return and intrusion into her life. It brought back even more painful memories. But intensity radiated from deep inside him, drawing her closer.

"Nikki." His low voice should have sounded like a growl, yet somehow she heard it as a deep caress, an effort to soothe her pain.

Pain he'd helped cause, she reminded herself. "I should go inside."

He nodded but didn't move, blocking entry to her home. "In a minute. I have one more question."

She curled her hands into tight fists and met his unwavering gaze. "Yes?"

"You had your one question. Now, I want mine. When you think about that night, what is it you remember most?"

He couldn't have stunned her more if he'd announced her brother was still alive. They'd danced around this subject but neither one of them dared broach it directly. Not since her stupid comment earlier, the one he'd all but ignored.

The reminder, now, added an edge to the sexual tension she'd been trying to fight the entire evening. Alone, in the dimly lit hall, the only noise the sound of their voices, all rational thought receded from her brain.

Her gaze never left his as she stepped forward. "You really want to know?"

"I wouldn't have asked otherwise."

She nodded and took two steps closer until she'd all but invaded his space. Having outmaneuvered herself, her body reacted in kind. A tight knot had settled in her stomach hours earlier and now unwound, sending sparks of desire throughout her body. She tingled from the inside out. From the pit of her stomach to her fingertips, energy and need surged through her... As if every fiber of her being recalled exactly what this man was capable of making her feel.

She swallowed hard. How could she react this way to the same person who'd used her and dumped her all within twenty-four hours? Her mind understood the facts. Her body didn't seem to care. Apparently neither did his because she noticed a slight hitch in his breathing, telling her he felt it, too.

"Tell me," he said.

"When I think about *that night*..." She purposefully emphasized her words and a muffled noise tore from deep in his throat.

She recognized the sound as one of desire. An answering tremor shook her and she squeezed her legs together in a futile effort to halt the waves of need he inspired. She wanted to give in to the moment but

she'd done that once before and suffered the consequences. Yet, when he reached for her, cupping her
face in his hand, she couldn't walk away and turned
her cheek into his embrace instead. Her eyelids fluttered closed and she let herself believe…

"Princess…"

She jerked back, fantasy gone, reality returning in
full force. No doubt, the name had the opposite effect
of what he'd intended. Nikki knew she had one chance
to make him understand what he'd done and she had
no intention of losing the opportunity.

"You want to know what I remember most about
that night?" she asked in a deceptively soft voice. "I
remember waking up naked and alone."

This time, he stiffened reflexively.

"I don't know what kind of game you're playing
with me, but you've already shown me how much you
care," she said. "One little fainting spell and a good
Samaritan gesture doesn't change a thing."

A muscle twitched beside his mouth, but he didn't
say a word, so she continued. "Now if you don't mind,
I'd like my keys and then I'd like to be alone." She
held out her hand and waited.

Tension reverberated between them. As his silence
continued, Nikki expected an explosion. Perhaps she
even wanted one – anything to give her the means to
relieve the building pressure.

When he finally answered, she was disappointed. "I don't play games." He spoke softly, with determination but not anger. "I promised Tony I'd look out for you. I may have done a lousy job so far, but that's about to change." He turned, inserted the key and pushed open the door. "Get some sleep." He stepped back to allow her inside.

She walked over the threshold, drawing into herself as she passed him, refusing to be lured back into the vortex of desire he effortlessly created. She stared into his ebony eyes. "I don't need a keeper."

"I disagree." His gaze raked over her and she knew if she looked into a mirror now, she'd cringe in disgust. Yet, she couldn't mistake the subtle darkening in his gaze and marveled that she could affect him still.

Not that it changed anything. Desire was a far cry from love and caring, and Nikki could accept no less for herself. She'd lost too many people in her life. She'd come too far to be just a charity case to the man she... *Damn.*

"Good night," he murmured. The door closed behind her with a soft click. She'd have preferred a loud slam.

Instead, he'd marched back into her life, turned her heart upside down once more, and retreated... all without a sound. He'd left her wound up and full of energy. Anger throbbed inside her, a rapid pulse that matched the beat of her heart. Tony had asked Kevin to look out for her? He intended to take care of her as if she were a child? The hell he was.

Nikki grabbed an overstuffed pillow and punched the center hard before sinking into the couch. She'd always been somebody's obligation. She'd been her parents' little girl, even after she'd graduated from high school and come East to college. Within the year, her parents had died in a fire and Tony, who had migrated to Boston long before, had become her surrogate parent. With Tony gone, Janine had assumed the role. Now Kevin wanted to get in on the act.

Well, she was an adult, though no one in her life had ever acknowledged that fact. Over these past couple of months, she'd proven she could take care of herself. She'd even found someone who was looking for a roommate at a rental she could afford if she scraped by.

She didn't need Kevin looking out for her. Nor did she want his pity. The only thing she'd ever wanted from him was the one thing she'd never have. She desired what her parents had enjoyed, what Tony and Janine had shared. And she respected herself too much to settle for less.

THREE

"Nikki." A hand shook her shoulder. "Nikki, wake up."

"What?" She jerked into a sitting position to find Janine standing over her, a concerned and motherly expression on her face. "Don't look at me like that," Nikki muttered.

"I can't help it. You're still in last night's work clothes, and you never made it to your room last night. You have dark circles under your eyes, and I'm worried." After folding the Afghan throw Nikki had used as a blanket the night before, Janine lowered herself onto the couch. Nikki glared at her.

"You should have thought of that before you brought Kevin back into my life. Where was your concern then?"

"I was thinking about you."

Nikki curled her legs beneath her. "Give me one

good reason why you did it. Just one. Make me understand how my best friend could betray me." Because she and Janine had seen each other through the aftermath of Tony's death and Kevin's abrupt disappearance, Janine knew how deeply Kevin had wounded her.

She would have given him her heart, if only he'd stuck around to accept it. He hadn't of course. She'd lost her brother and Kevin in rapid succession.

Janine met Nikki's gaze. No remorse showed in her green-eyed gaze. None shadowed her expression. Only the kindness and compassion she'd shown Nikki from the start. "Would you have preferred a gentle let-down the morning after?"

"Whose side are you on anyway?"

"Yours." Janine laid a hand on her shoulder. "Always yours. What Kevin did was wrong, but did you ever think he was suffering, too?" she asked softly.

"Yes." And Nikki had wanted to help him heal.

"You couldn't have healed him. He had to come back on his own," Janine said, reading her mind.

"With a little nudging from you?" The only person she had left had switched sides, leaving her to fend for herself. Nikki didn't understand. The world had shifted beneath her feet and she hated the unsteady sensation that left her wondering what jarring thing would come next.

"He'd already come back, settled into a house he inherited," Janine said.

He'd admitted as much, Nikki thought. "And?"

"And I asked him to meet me at the bar."

"Why?"

"Because when I'm gone, you're going to need someone to lean on."

Nikki bristled at the implication that she couldn't take care of herself. Coming from the person who'd seen her at her worst then seen her pull her life together after, the lack of faith hurt And then the rest of Janine's words sunk in. "What do you mean, when you're gone?"

"My baby needs more than me." Janine placed her hand over her still-flat stomach, rubbing circles in a gesture that had become familiar to Nikki during the past few months. "Actually, I need more than me, and no insult to you because I'm going to miss you like crazy, but I need my family."

Nikki blinked at the sudden but not altogether un-expected admission. She'd seen the signs lately—the increased phone calls home, and Janine's recollections of the farmhouse in Iowa where she'd grown up.

"Okay." What else could she say that wouldn't be selfish and one-sided? She loved Janine like a sister. Losing her would be like losing Tony all over again. But she understood and would respect her decision.

She had no choice. "There are always airplanes and holidays. I'm not going to let my niece or nephew grow up without knowing me."

Janine smiled. "I'd come back to visit for the same reason. Meantime, I'm leaving you in the lurch with no roommate."

Nikki shook her head. "You'd never do that. Look, I can't afford the rent here, but there's this other waitress who's looking for a roommate, and I can afford that on what I make at the bar. See? I'll be fine and you didn't need to worry about me.

"I can't believe you're taking this so well."

"I can't believe you didn't think I would. Look at me, Janine. I've grown up."

"Yes, you have." Her sister-in-law's gaze traveled over her. "How are you feeling this morning?"

"Better than last…" Nikki's words trailed off. "How did you know I was sick?"

"Kevin called. I grabbed the phone before it could wake you."

"Well, he shouldn't have bothered. I'm fine now."

"Are you?"

"What's that supposed to mean?"

"Just that there have been other signs that…"

A loud pounding at the door stopped whatever Janine had been about to say. "I'll get it," Janine said.

"Signs that what?" Nikki called after her.

"Never mind," the other woman muttered. "You'll figure it out soon enough."

"Who is it?" she called, preventing Nikki from questioning her further.

"Kevin."

Nikki's stomach did another forward roll, just as it had last night in the bar. Janine opened the door.

Nikki met his gaze. Same black leather jacket, same razor stubble, same handsome features. The same man who turned her insides to mush with a glance. He strolled inside, whistling as if he hadn't a care in the world.

Nikki wished her own emotions were as controlled and steady when he was around. She probably had nothing to worry about. Knowing Kevin, he'd have his say and disappear. In the meantime, she had Janine as a buffer.

Nikki forced a smile.

Janine gave him a brotherly hug. "Good to see you again, Kevin. Unfortunately, I was on my way out."

Nikki narrowed her gaze. Janine picked up her purse that was hanging over a chair, grabbed her keys from the counter, and avoided Nikki's gaze as she made her way to the door. Her sister-in-law had awakened her, dropped her bomb, and left her alone with Kevin. It didn't take a genius to figure out she'd been set up again.

The door slammed shut and Kevin turned toward her. For the first time, she noticed the brown bag in his hand.

She ran a hand down her tangled mass of hair. She didn't relish him seeing her looking like last night's garbage.

"What do you want?" she asked him. The sooner she found out, the sooner she could get rid of him. She could use a hot shower and catch a few decent hours of sleep in her own bed before the Saturday night shift began.

"To settle things between us once and for all."

Nikki shrugged. "Funny, I thought we already had."

He didn't answer, just thrust out the hand with the innocuous-looking bag.

She grabbed it and peered inside. Her stomach rolled once more, only this time she had a better hunch as to the cause. "Home pregnancy test?"

"Take it and then we'll talk."

The command was insulting, the possibility frightening. She'd just discovered she was losing her apartment. She'd counted on her bartending job to hold her over for the time being, until she could save enough to finish her semester of student teaching while holding down a part-time job that didn't leave her wiped out in the morning. Pregnant women didn't waitress in a cocktail bar.

Pregnant women… Was it possible? *They hadn't used protection*, she thought, recalling every intimate detail of her time with Kevin. She swallowed hard, then mentally counted months. Nikki began to shake as she realized anything was possible. Since that night, she hadn't had a spare second to worry about anything except getting to work on time and sleeping enough to serve drinks again the next night. But there was the frequent nausea, the dizziness… not unlike when her parents had died, but much more persistent.

She couldn't be certain. She met his steady gaze. "Even if I am pregnant, which I doubt, it's not your concern." It was hers, she thought, her fear mounting.

"You're wrong."

"We shared one night, Kevin. It's over."

He shook his head slowly. "Princess, I have a hunch that night was just the beginning."

* * *

Nikki hoped, with everything in her, that Kevin was wrong. Her hand went to her lower abdomen and molded around her flat stomach. Or did she? She'd gone to college because she'd believed in being able to support herself. She'd chosen education because she loved children. Teaching had been a way to be around kids until she was able to fulfill her dream of having a family of her own.

Only financial considerations had forced her to put her education on hold. Although having a baby was a dream come true, the timing couldn't be worse. She was barely supporting herself. In no way could she afford to care for another tiny human being.

A child. Hers and Kevin's. Nikki's hand curled around the pink, blue, and white box. It was time to find out. "I'll be back." She took two steps forward, when he called out to her.

"Nikki."

She turned.

"Forget what happened in the past. If you're pregnant, I'll be there."

She couldn't answer. Not yet. Because her dreams of children had always included two parents and a loving home. The kind she and Tony had grown up in. Kevin would support her; she didn't doubt his word. True, he'd left after their one night, but no promises had been exchanged. He was a man of honor, despite what had passed between them. He'd be there for her now just as he said... but only because she was having his baby. *Not because he loved her.*

Kevin could provide the two-parent home of her dreams, but the warmth, love, caring, and devotion would be missing. She pushed back the nausea that seemed to be her constant companion and locked herself in the bathroom.

If she was pregnant, she'd be someone's obligation once more. Worse, she'd be Kevin's obligation, tolerated because of a baby they'd created, but not loved for herself. Oh, God. She wanted him, but not like that.

She opened the flaps on the side of the box. A quick read of the instructions, and easy compliance. She glanced at her watch. In three minutes she'd know. Nikki lowered herself onto the closed toilet seat and chewed on her thumbnail.

"Is it time?" His voice sounded from outside the bathroom door.

She drew an unsteady breath. Though she'd prefer to be alone when she found out, Kevin had as much right to know the results as she did. And she might as well not suffer these agonizing minutes by herself. "Come on in."

The door opened and he walked into the small bathroom she shared with Janine. His gaze flew to the white stick lying on the counter top by the sink. "Well?"

She glanced at her watch. "Two more minutes."

He propped one shoulder against the wall. Silence surrounded them and tension flowed thick until she couldn't take another second. "What are you doing with yourself now that you're back?" she asked. Maybe normal conversation would make the time pass more quickly. "I know you haven't returned to the force, at least not yet."

He shrugged. "I took a job with an old friend, as an in-house security consultant for his manufacturing company."

She looked up, surprised that the man, who'd always made his job his life, had given it up. "And you enjoy the monotony after all those years as a detective?"

He shrugged. "It's a living. How much longer?" he asked, obviously changing the subject away from himself.

"You know what they say… a watched pot never boils." She forced a strained laugh, then glanced at the watch on her wrist. "Another thirty seconds." The blood drained from her head, leaving her weak.

"Hang on," he murmured. "Now tell me why you gave up teaching."

She smiled, grateful for his sensitivity at this particular moment in time. She splayed her fingers over her jeans. "I had one semester of student teaching left and that's a full-time obligation. I couldn't possibly work nights, formulate lesson plans and be my best the following day," she explained. "Tony was going to help me out for the semester and I was going to pay him back once I started working full-time. But he…"

She swallowed a painful sob before continuing. "He died. The small amount of money my parents had left me was almost gone, Janine was pregnant…" She shook her head. "Everything changed overnight."

"And it's about to change again. Thanks to me."

She shook her head, found herself reaching for his hand despite better judgment. His palm felt warm and dry in hers. "I never did understand why you blamed yourself. I read the reports. You weren't in the car, Tony got the call, you had your radio on, but he took off before you…"

"Before I got downstairs. If I'd been in the car, he wouldn't have had the chance to play renegade cop. I knew him well enough to know what he'd do and I ignored my gut… If I'd been in the damn car, he'd have had backup. He wouldn't have been killed."

Nikki lowered her eyes. She shook her head slowly. "Things happen for a reason, Kevin. It was his time. He knew the risks, knew better than to drive off and leave you behind. *He should have waited for you.*"

"And I should have been there sooner… Damn it, there's no point in rehashing the past."

She exhaled a resigned sigh. "You're right. Especially when the future awaits." Her gaze darted to the stick on the counter.

He released her hand only long enough to reach out and tip her chin up. Her gaze met his. "It'll be okay."

"Easy for you to say."

"Now take a look."

With shaking hands, she uncovered one end of the long, thin stick. She didn't have to look for confirmation of what she already knew. They'd created a life. Together, they would have to deal with that.

But how? Kevin knew nothing about family, and intimacy had caused him to run far and fast. She couldn't expect him to welcome this turn of events.

"It'll be okay," he said again.

A tear leaked from one corner of her eye. She brushed at the moisture with her sleeve. "Would you stop saying that?" Needing time alone, she scrambled past him, heading through the door and into the living area without looking back.

"Where are you going?" he called after her.

"I have to shower and get some sleep before my shift starts again." She worked in a frenzy, pausing to pick up stray socks, shoes and her purse.

"We have to talk."

"Later. First I have a job to do, then I need time to think."

"About what?"

She whirled around to face him. "That's a stupid question. You might have figured out I was pregnant yesterday, but I had no idea until two seconds ago.

And you ask me what I need to think about?" Her voice rose in pitch and her palms covered her stomach in a new movement, but one she was sure to become intimately familiar with in due time.

He exhaled hard. "Take the night off."

"Impossible. I can't afford it."

"I can."

"You're not responsible for me, Kevin."

"I promised Tony I'd take care of you and you're having my child. That makes me responsible."

She hugged her clothes tight against her chest and met his gaze with a steady one of her own. "That's what I was afraid of." Before he could answer, she hit the bathroom running, slamming the door shut behind her.

* * *

Nikki made herself a promise. She'd concentrate on her job tonight, and take tomorrow and Monday, her days off, to deal with the fact that she was pregnant. With Kevin's baby. A fuzzy warmth curled through her stomach at the thought, one at odds with the truth of her life. She shook her head, refusing to think about him now.

But not thinking of Kevin was like having someone tell you not to think about images of nice things—like weekends, vacations, or summertime. The harder you tried, the more they danced in front of your eyes, teased your senses, and invaded your dreams.

She walked over to her most recent table: men who'd come to the bar for a night on the town. She recognized them as regulars—lawyers who frequented the bar after work and occasionally on the weekends. They knew how to flirt and have a good time, but despite the banter, they were harmless. In another life, she might even have been interested.

A life that didn't include Kevin Manning, maybe.

"Can I get you fellas something?" Nikki asked.

"Nachos and beer."

"Vodka, straight up."

"You, honey," a good-looking blonde-haired man said. Leaning back in his chair, he stretched his arm out so his fingers touched her waist. She forced herself to remain in place. The more amiable she was, the better her tip. Right now, she needed all the spare cash she could possibly earn each night.

Besides, this same guy had made overtures before. Her responses had always been the same: a polite but firm *no*. He expected it and flirted anyway. No harm, no foul, she thought. She could handle him.

She forced a smile. "Sorry. I'm not on the menu," she said and took a step backward. "But nice try."

He grinned. "Too bad. We could have a good time."

No, we couldn't. Because he wasn't Kevin. Her heart belonged to Kevin Manning from the minute he'd claimed her as his own. A primitive notion, Nikki knew. But valid anyway.

Too bad he didn't reciprocate her feelings. Then this pregnancy would be the answer to her prayers. In a funny way, it still was. How could she regret fate, or the life growing inside her?

Unfortunately, nothing was as simple as she'd like it to be. Which brought her back to her dilemma. No health insurance, no job once she started to show, and no valid means of support or daycare for her child. So much for dealing with tomorrow, Nikki thought.

She made her way back to the bar, following the same routine of previous nights. The pounding beat of rock music combined with the heavy sheen of smoke and the accompanying foul odors of cigars, cigarettes, and liquor worked against her. Nikki picked up the tray of drinks and tried holding her breath until she reached a semblance of fresh air away from the bar. The effort was futile, only serving to make the dizziness and nausea worse.

Good, Lord, why did they call it *morning sickness?* She paused at the table of men once more to empty her tray and defray another halfhearted attempt to arrange a date. The way things were going, it was destined to be a very long night.

*   *   *

Kevin stood with his back against the wall, nursing the same soda for the last hour. He didn't want to call attention to himself by ordering another drink. He told himself he wanted to keep an eye on Nikki in case she had another fainting spell. That was part truth and part bull. He also wanted to keep an eye on the male customers with wandering eyes, roving hands, and too much testosterone. If the blonde suit laid another hand on her while she served him his drink, Kevin would dump the guy's beer in his lap himself.

He told himself he didn't like seeing any woman harassed. This was true. He'd seen his lecherous father in action too many times, and had dragged his sorry, drunken butt home too often... sometimes before, sometimes after he'd offended the lady in question. But the truth tonight went way deeper than the issue of sexual harassment.

Kevin didn't want another guy laying a hand on Nikki. She was carrying his child. That gave him the right to keep her safe. This child gave him chance to do something right in his life. He had no idea how to be a parent or a husband. But no way was he about to blow his responsibilities.

Not with this woman. Not again. Just watching her bar routine sent a surge of something raw and primitive flowing through his veins. For the first time since he was an angry kid, he wanted to lash out and hit someone for attempting to take what was his. The thought made him laugh… because Nikki Welles was many things – including pregnant – but she wasn't his.

FOUR

Three days with no word. Kevin figured he'd given Nikki enough time to digest her situation. She hadn't called and he hadn't expected her to. He had, however, had enough of the silent treatment.

He entered the familiar building and walked up the three flights of stairs. The dark stairwell with its many steps was another reason why he wasn't comfortable with Nikki staying on here after Janine was gone. His rambling house with its many rooms on the ground level would be more comfortable for Nikki. And more difficult for him. Sharing a home with her would give him glimpses of warmth and the illusion of a family... He didn't deserve either.

He knocked on the door and waited. No answer. Kevin banged again, louder this time. Janine was at work, but Nikki didn't hold a day job. He'd chosen to arrive before nine, before Nikki would be out for the day. He leaned closer to the door and listened. Still silent. He banged again.

An uncomfortable prickle of fear worked on his nerves. Even if she'd been asleep, his pounding would have awakened her by now. He had no reason to believe anything was wrong... except she'd fainted once before. He had a hunch she wasn't feeling as well as she claimed. What if she'd gotten dizzy again? What if she'd passed out cold on the floor, or worse, in the shower?

What if, like Tony, she was alone and something was wrong and he was too late? Kevin didn't hesitate. He jimmied the lock and tore inside the apartment. The empty apartment, he realized as he glanced around and hit every room, checking the beds, the couch, and the floors.

Feeling like a fool, Kevin made his way into the kitchen and lowered himself onto one of the bar stools. He'd obviously overreacted. Though his adrenaline still flowed fast and his heart still pounded against his chest, he forced himself to breathe deeply. Part of him felt like an ass, breaking into the apartment on a whim. And part of him still felt uneasy.

He ran his fingers through his hair, attempting to calm his raging nerves. So Nikki had gone out early. He was sure he could count a number of places open at this hour, but he couldn't discount the nagging feeling in his gut that something was off.

He looked around the impeccably clean apartment, seeing nothing unusual or out of place. Until his gaze fell to the open telephone book on the kitchen counter.

Planned Parenthood.

His worst fear was confirmed.

When Nikki had found out about the pregnancy, she'd said she needed time to think. Kevin had convinced himself she meant about how to deal with her altered future. But what if she'd spent the weekend thinking about whether she wanted this baby at all? Though Nikki loved life and children, she'd suffered enough in the last few months to have a skewed perception of reality. And the one person she ought to turn to, the baby's father, had already proved he couldn't be trusted when things got heated or emotional.

What if, feeling alone and abandoned, she turned to the one option she'd surely regret later? The one option he regretted now? Planned or not, Kevin was responsible for the life growing inside her and he was responsible for Nikki as well.

With a second glance at the phone book and address, in a part of town he would never allow her to frequent alone, he jumped from the stool and left the apartment, hitting the street at a dead run.

*   *   *

Nikki wrapped the white sheet around her naked body and waited for the doctor's return. The sterile room felt cold and empty, unlike her heart, which was warm and full of more hope than she'd had in awhile. She pressed a hand against her flat stomach.

A child. Kevin's child, yes, but it was her baby, her hope. Her future. Once the shock had worn off, she'd examined the difficulties that lay ahead and despite the fear and uncertainty, she acknowledged a flurry of nervous excitement as well.

"Sorry, I had an emergency phone call." The young female doctor entered the room, wheeling a small machine behind her.

Nikki smiled. "That's okay. You already gave me the news I was expecting… I mean the news I was expecting to hear."

The doctor laughed. "Either way, sounds about right to me. Your examination was fine. Nothing unusual. But I'd like to verify the due date and check some other things with an ultrasound." Nikki wanted to tell her there was no need to worry about the accuracy of her due date. She'd been with one man, one time. And she'd never forget.

"Ready?" the woman asked with a smile.

Nikki was grateful for the doctor's warm manner and youth. The sheer terror she'd felt upon entering the building for basic prenatal care had evaporated under this woman's caring ministrations. Although she couldn't say what she'd expected from a phone book-picked clinic, Nikki was thankful for what she'd found.

The doctor shifted the white sheet until the opening fell to Nikki's back. "Before I do an ultrasound, I want to remind you, we've already discussed your options and though you've made your feelings clear, you need to remember something."

"What's that?" Nikki asked, although she could barely concentrate on anything except the thought of seeing her baby for the first time. Excitement and trepidation rippled in her stomach.

The doctor angled the machine closer to the examining table. "You have a limited window of opportunity, should you decide to terminate the pregnancy. Now…" She glanced at Nikki and smiled. "You ready?"

A loud knock sounded at the door. Nikki sat up straighter, grabbing for the sheet that covered too little.

Dr. Molloy shot Nikki an apologetic glance. "Must be an emergency. Let me just check." She rose from her seat and walked to the door, opening it enough for her to slip outside.

Seconds later, the doctor returned. "There's someone who insists on seeing you," she said to Nikki.

"Who…"

"Nicole?" Kevin's voice sounded in the hallway.

Shock rippled through her. Nikki glanced down at the sheet and, seeing she was as decently covered as she could be under the circumstances, she nodded to the doctor. Kevin barged around the doctor and Nikki found herself facing an obviously upset man.

Dr. Molloy placed herself between Nikki and Kevin, as though she believed Nikki needed protection. Given his flashing obsidian eyes, which would intimidate anyone, even on a good day, Nikki didn't blame the other woman for her concern.

"This is highly irregular," she said.

This whole situation was highly irregular, but her personal life wasn't the doctor's concern. "I realize that," Nikki murmured.

"Who is this man?"

"He's…" She sought for a diplomatic way to describe her relationship with Kevin. Somehow the term lover no longer fit, boyfriend was too immature for what they'd once shared, and future anything was out of the question… for many reasons.

"The baby's father." Kevin supplied the answer Nikki had both sought and fought to avoid at the same time. His words were a painful reminder she would be tied to him forever, but never bonded in love or caring. Merely out of necessity.

He took a step farther into the room.

"That doesn't give you the right to charge in here." The pleasant doctor had taken on the role of guard and protector, a part Nikki sensed the woman played often in this place.

Kevin drew a deep breath, searching for what Nikki believed was a semblance of control. He stuffed his hands into his pockets and turned that dark gaze her way.

Her stomach pitched, having nothing to do with morning sickness. The harsh angles and planes in his face and the razor stubble on his cheeks were enough to make any woman weak, but the look in his eyes struck Nikki in the heart. They reflected inner torment and pain.

She sucked in a startled breath. Heaven help her, but she was still dangerously drawn to this man and the vulnerable part of him he hid from view. The part she'd glimpsed so thoroughly their one night together.

"I can call nine-one-one." The doctor glanced at Nikki.

Kevin's gaze narrowed. "Tell her, Nicole."

She clutched her fingers around the cold sheet, feeling more exposed and defenseless than ever before. "He's the baby's father," she said, confirming his story.

He clenched his jaw and she knew she hadn't gone

far enough to please him. Tough. Pleasing him wasn't on today's agenda. Taking her life one step at a time was.

"Like I said, Mr...."

"Manning," he said.

"Mr. Manning. Paternity doesn't give you the right to barge in here. Now either you leave, or..."

"No."

At the sound of Nikki's voice, both Kevin and the doctor turned. "Can you give us a minute?" Nikki asked the startled doctor.

"As long as you're sure. You don't have to talk to him."

"I want to." Relief and gratitude flickered for a brief second in Kevin's gaze before the steely resolve returned.

Good, Nikki thought. She'd much rather deal with his obstinate side than any veneer of caring he chose to present in order to get his way. She wasn't at risk of turning into a marshmallow when he was his take-charge self. As long as she wasn't faced with the softer Kevin Manning, she'd be okay.

"I'll be back in five minutes," the doctor said, in what seemed like a warning.

This behavior wasn't like the Kevin she knew. Something must have triggered his anger—or fear, she thought glancing into his eyes. She knew Kevin would never hurt her, at least not intentionally, but this woman couldn't know that. And Nikki wondered how many of the opposite situations the doctor saw every day. The thought saddened her.

Deep down, Kevin was a good man. Not *the* man for her, though. And that hurt even more. He'd take the obligation of a baby seriously, but he'd never let himself see her as more than his responsibility. She'd never be the woman he loved. She wondered if he'd ever had experience with the word. Recalling his mention of a drunken father, she had her doubts. But she couldn't let them sway her because their connection was now iron-clad.

Her palm came to rest against her belly. She'd be dealing with him for years to come and if she didn't assert herself now, she'd pay later. Just because she carried his child didn't give him license to control her or the situation—no matter how strong the obligation he felt towards Tony or this baby. It was time the ex-cop learned Nikki was a big girl with a mind of her own.

"Five minutes," the doctor said again, then turned and followed the receptionist out the door.

Nikki watched them leave, marshaling whatever reserved strength she could muster before dealing with Kevin. She sensed she would need it.

No sooner had the doctor's white coat disappeared

than Kevin slammed the door closed behind him. Nikki jumped at the unusually loud sound.

"What are you doing here, Kevin?" Knowing a strong offense was the best defense, Nikki didn't give him a chance to strike first.

"I should think that would be obvious."

"What's obvious to me is that you've barged in on me in a private place in a private situation and acted like an arrogant man who believes he has rights where he really has none."

Contrition flashed in his eyes. He was across the room in two long strides. "You scared me half to death. I show up at your door before nine expecting to find you home, and you're not. I figured you were out cold on the floor and when I break in to check…"

"You broke in?"

"I thought you'd passed out, Nicole. I thought you needed help." Did his voice shake or was it her imagination?

So she'd been right. Fear motivated his actions. Her heart did a crazy flip at the thought of Kevin's concern. Caring was a possible start, one that could lead to more…to love… couldn't it? Her hand clutched around her stomach. "And you're here now because…"

"Because I was hoping we could talk before you went ahead and aborted my child!"

Nikki sucked in an obviously startled breath. When Kevin had seen the clinic address in the phone book, he'd panicked. Not only for Nikki's health, but also for the welfare of his baby. Although he'd made mistakes in the past he took this responsibility seriously. She was startled to realize he wanted this child.

"I know it's your body and your choice," Kevin said, forestalling any argument she might make. "But I helped create this new life and I deserve to be a part of any decisions you make… before they're irreparable."

* * *

Her eyes flashed brilliant sparks, but he couldn't read what was going on in her head. "Please turn around."

"I'm not walking out that door until we talk."

"I agree. Now turn around and give me a chance to get decent," she muttered.

Kevin forcibly pushed down the adrenaline that had been flowing since discovering the phone book on her counter, and focused on Nicole instead. Dark hair brushed her bare shoulders and she sat clutching a white sheet that threatened to fall. Beneath it, she wasn't dressed. He knew what curves lay under the draped sheet and knew what effect they'd had on him in the past. What effect they had on him now.

For the first time, he took in the private situation he'd intruded upon and cringed. He hadn't given the circumstances a thought. He pivoted toward the door, giving her the respect he'd denied her before. And he waited.

The rustling sound of cotton shifting and gliding over her naked skin was pure torture and almost enough to make him forget he had anger and issues of his own.

"That's a major conclusion you jumped to." Her voice whispered close to his ear and a light hint of vanilla fragrance wafted in the air.

He turned. She'd come up behind him, still wearing the sheet, although now it was draped tight around her like a sarong. Her fingers gripped the edges, clutching onto the ends hard and fast.

"Do you blame me? You do realize you're standing undressed in a Planned Parenthood examining room?"

Deep purple eyes gazed at him in dismay and disappointment. "Is that what you think of me? Forgetting the one night that created this baby? You were closer to my family than anyone else. You ignored football to listen to my hopes and dreams of being a teacher, of being a mother one day."

Her voice caught and Kevin's stomach lurched in response.

"You of all people know how many losses I've suffered in the past few years. Both my parents, my brother, and…" She halted without warning, but the tension was obvious in the set of her shoulders and the flush in her cheeks.

She was right, Kevin realized. In all his mulling over the angles of this situation, he'd never factored Nikki's past into the equation. How *could* he think she'd willingly get rid of her own child? He'd kick himself if he could.

How much more pain would he cause her? "Go on," he said softly, hoping to somehow calm her down. Distress couldn't be good for the baby or its mother.

"Forget it." She blinked at the moisture forming in her eyes. A lone tear trickled down her face and the truth settled in his gut.

He could do many things. Forgetting what she'd been about to say wasn't one of them. "You were listing your losses. Your parents, Tony... and who else?"

"Janine," she said quickly, averting her gaze.

"True, but it's not who you meant." Kevin had no desire to torture her any more than he wanted to bring the issue to light. But if he and Nikki didn't resolve their night together once and for all, her pain, resentment, and anger would eat her alive.

He might deserve to be horsewhipped for leaving her, but she needed to expunge her anger. Then they'd have to find a way to go on.

He placed a finger beneath her chin and raised her head until their eyes met. "Who else, Nicole?"

"You," she spat. "You left me, too." Eyes blazing, cheeks also on fire, yet Nikki held her own. He was proud of her. Maybe they'd come to terms with each other yet.

"And each time you say or do something like this…" She gestured around the sterile room. "You tear me apart all over again. I won't have it, Kevin. Do you want to know why I'm here?"

Not trusting himself to speak, he merely nodded.

"For prenatal care. Where else would I go for basic visits? I don't have insurance, I can't afford a private doctor…" Her shoulders shook as she spoke, testament to the effort this confrontation was taking.

He knew how difficult this trip must have been for her alone. He'd had a hell of a time finding the clinic and he wasn't afraid to venture down side streets and alleys.

He wrapped an arm around her and led her back to the examining table. Her soft skin brushed his fingers, and her tantalizing scent touched his heart. She sat down and inhaled deeply.

She had enough strength for both of them, he thought. He took some of her courage and drew it into himself. From now on, though, she'd lean on him. He'd see to it.

"If you'd been willing to sit down with me and talk, we could have resolved some of those issues instead of you having to turn to clinical care. Alone."

"Why would I sit down with you? You walked out once. Even if you're here to stay now, and for the record, I believe you are—"

"You do?"

She sighed. "You're a good man, Kevin. That's half the problem. You'll be here for the baby. I know you wouldn't abandon your child. But there's no way in hell I'll rely on you again."

Before he could respond, the door creaked open on old hinges. "Everything okay in here?" the doctor asked.

"Yes," Nikki answered.

"Then if you don't mind, we have to get started. I have patients waiting and I'm running late as it is."

"Come on in." He spared a glance at Nikki's pale, drawn face.

"Weren't you just leaving?" she asked.

He shook his head. "It's *our* baby's heartbeat, Nicole. I'm not going anywhere."

* * *

Nikki had protested, but Kevin drove her home from the clinic. They drove in silence. Given the many confusing thoughts she was having, she figured he was lost in thought, too.

When they passed by one of the local colleges, Nikki's gaze was drawn to the wide-open spaces and people milling about. "I'd like to get out here."

"Here?" He slowed the car. "Why?"

"I need air, space, time to think. I want to walk and feel the breeze against my face. I want to deal with everything I've learned in the last couple of days. Alone," she added softly.

He hesitated, but slowed the car even more.

"I'm an adult. I can take a walk and grab the subway home. I can even take a cab if it makes you feel better, but please give me the space and respect I need."

He pulled into the first open space on the side of the road. "Do you have money on you?"

"Do you think I'm a complete incompetent? I'll be fine. I just want some time."

He nodded. "Then you've got it."

"Thank you." She got out of the car, slamming the door behind her. She didn't look back to see if Kevin watched or pulled away.

She walked for an hour on the Boston Common, watching the college kids alternatively lounging and studying by the water. Young and carefree. She used to be like them. She shook her head. She'd been one of them, yes. But like them? Maybe not. She'd always felt older than her years—due in part to the constant need to challenge her family's concept that she was their baby.

And now she was having one of her own. With her hand over her stomach, she turned and headed toward the T—Boston's subway system—to take her home. She took her seat and the ride passed in a blur, as she was still dazed by the morning at the clinic, and the sonogram picture in her purse.

No sooner did she get inside the apartment building and up the stairs, when what sounded like hammering reached her ears. She rounded the corner and came to her apartment. Curious, she walked faster.

She headed down the hall to find her door open wide, and Kevin on his knees, tools spread around him as he worked to replace the lock he'd damaged during his earlier break-in.

She came up behind him and leaned close. The heavenly scent of aftershave assaulted her senses. "Hi," she whispered in his ear.

He jumped back and the screwdriver went flying out of his hand. "Damn, you shouldn't sneak up on someone like that. Especially a man with a sharp object," he muttered.

Nikki grinned, happy to have gotten the upper hand, even over something so trivial. It gave her hope for the future.

He grabbed for the wayward screwdriver. "The least you could do is say thank you," he muttered.

"Thank you. But I'd be remiss if I didn't point out that I wouldn't need the lock changed if someone hadn't overreacted."

"Don't remind me."

She stepped around him, intending to head inside her apartment. Instead she turned and knelt down beside him. "We have to come to some sort of agreement. A meeting of the minds."

"What kind of agreement?" he asked.

"You have to let me live my life," she said, thinking of their earlier argument in the doctor's office.

The one revolving around her keeping her job. Thank goodness the doctor had agreed with Nikki—as long as she felt up to it and there were no signs of distress, she could continue working.

"I wish it were that simple, Princess."

She shut her eyes against the sound of his voice and *that* word. "It's as simple as you make it. I'm keeping my job."

He nodded, probably recalling that the battle lines had been drawn. "Then I'll be keeping an eye on you."

It did figure. The one time she didn't want Kevin around, he had no intention of leaving. She'd just have to ignore his presence in her life, as difficult as she knew it would be.

She was responsible for herself and the life growing inside her. She welcomed the challenge. She just wished Kevin didn't feel the same.

She sighed, knowing she'd better get used to his presence. He wasn't going anywhere.

FIVE

Sunlight streamed through the blinds in Nikki's bedroom. She'd managed to toss and turn all afternoon, but she'd gotten no sleep. The night shift loomed long ahead of her. Nikki pulled on her boots, then had to rest until the exhaustion subsided.

"Why don't you take the night off?" Janine stood in the doorway to Nikki's room.

"Because I need every dollar I can make." Nikki glanced up from her seat on the bed. "So tell me how long you knew?"

Janine shrugged. "Awhile. But until you were ready to face what your body was telling you, I figured I was better off keeping my mouth shut."

"And bringing Kevin back into my life."

"He's the baby's father."

"And I would have told him—once I figured it out for myself. Right now, I have no breathing room." In

75

fact, if she allowed herself, Nikki thought she'd suffocate from the entire situation. "I have no time to think about the best way to handle things because he's trying to take control."

Janine walked into the room, her sneakers squeaking against the hardwood floor as she moved toward Nikki. "And this is a bad thing?" She parked herself beside Nikki on the down comforter on the bed. "If a man wants to help take care of you, I say you should let him."

Forcing a deep breath, Nikki gathered her thoughts before trying to explain. Nikki and Janine weren't all that different in what they wanted out of life. Family and happiness. It wasn't that Janine wanted or even needed a man to take care of her. She could take care of herself, but the natural extension of *caring*—the loving—that was what Janine lost when Tony died.

What Nikki would never have with Kevin. "You're mistaking what Kevin feels for me. Obligation isn't love. A sense of responsibility isn't caring. Oh, I know he cares about me, but it isn't enough." She met Janine's concerned gaze. "Tell me something. Would you have stayed with Tony if he'd gotten you pregnant but wasn't in love with you? If you couldn't share all those special times? The ones that are getting you through the pain now?"

Nikki grabbed for her sister-in-law's hand. Janine

had to understand, if only because Nikki was tired and needed the strength of someone else's understanding, at least for one night.

"No, I wouldn't have stayed with him. But apparently I have more faith in Kevin than you do. Or at least in his feelings." Janine sighed. "The same way you didn't know you were pregnant despite all the obvious signs? He just hasn't gotten in touch with his feelings. Yet."

"Ever the optimist." Nikki marveled at her sister-in-law's strength.

Janine smiled. "When you have another life to think of first, it's amazing how your perception of the world changes. You'll see."

Nikki nodded. "I agree with you." Her hand went to her still-flat stomach. "But it's because of this life that I have to be realistic. And counting on Kevin for more than fatherhood won't do either of us any good."

"I'm going to make myself something to eat," Janine said and rose from the bed. "You know, Nicole, you're very much like your brother. You see things one way: your way." She shook her head, sadness etched in her features and the dejected tilt of her head. "But what happens if that tunnel vision of yours is wrong—and you count out the very people you ought to believe in?"

Nikki narrowed her eyes. "What are you saying?"

"That as well as you knew your brother, you didn't know him at all. Because it's too hard to see likenesses that you don't want to face. And he didn't trust enough. Not in me, not in his partner…"

"Tony trusted Kevin with his life," Nikki argued. But she was unsure if it was her brother she was defending or Kevin and his lack of faith in himself. He believed he'd failed Tony. Nikki couldn't bear it if Janine felt the same way.

Janine shook her head. "Tony trusted Kevin as much as he trusted anyone. Unfortunately, it wasn't saying much. He shouldn't have left Kevin behind that night and you know it."

Nikki nodded. If her brother had waited for his partner, he might be alive today. "But I don't get how Tony's behavior applies to me."

"No, you don't. And I hope you never will."

Nikki decided to leave Janine's riddles alone. She was too tired to make sense of them now anyway. "What are your plans?" Nikki asked.

"I'm booked on a flight at the end of the week. I want to go home and get my bearings. Decide where I want to live before I pack my things and worry about moving them."

"I'll help any way I can. You know that."

"I do and I appreciate it. Most I can handle alone,

but Tony's things…" Janine's voice cracked with emotion and she drew a deep breath before continuing. "When I get back, will you help me sort through them?"

Nikki nodded, knowing it would take the strength of two people to tackle that job and was glad she had a few weeks reprieve.

* * *

The bar music had reached its crescendo. Kevin took a sip of soda and wondered if he was getting old or if it was the scene before him he'd grown tired of. One week of hanging out in the bar, watching Nikki do her thing, was getting to him. Each night, her steps grew heavier, her pace slower, her smile dimmer. And each night he had to sit on his hands while she worked, anything to prevent him from picking her up and physically hauling her out of the bar.

He dug into his pocket and came up with the small black and white printout of the sonogram depicting the baby. *His* baby, his and Nikki's. His heart beat faster in his chest and a lump formed in the back of his throat. Such a tiny little thing. Minute in size but so heavy a burden. He shook his head. Not a burden, a responsibility. A commitment. One he took both seriously and willingly. Whether he could live up to it was another story.

He'd do his damndest to see he didn't fail again. Last week at Planned Parenthood, he'd voiced his misgivings regarding Nikki's continued employment. The doctor had informed him Nikki wasn't sick, she was pregnant. In fact, the good doctor hadn't objected to Nikki's job unless she sacrificed her health in any way. At the time, Kevin swore to Nicole he'd back off the waitressing issue. To himself, he'd promised he'd maintain a steady vigil and step in at the first sign of problems or distress.

No way he'd let her end up like his mother—overworked, manhandled, and dead way too young.

He glanced up. Nikki leaned against the back wall behind the bar. For support or a second's rest, Kevin couldn't guess. But he knew, even if Nikki didn't, that she'd just worked her last shift.

*　　*　　*

Nikki reached for her jacket just as she heard her name being called. She turned to find Jack, the owner and her boss standing in the doorframe leading to his office. She sighed, grabbed her coat anyway and headed for the closet-sized room from which he ran his domain. Since her interview, where he'd grilled her on her nonexistent skills, she'd managed to steer clear of his mulish personality by not dropping the glasses onto the floor. Her crash-course courtesy of the other employees had saved her more than once.

"You wanted to see me?"

He nodded. "We have a problem."

"I can't imagine what that would be," she said in her most compliant voice. "What's wrong?"

He chewed on the end of the expensive cigar. "I can't keep you on."

She clutched her fingers around the material of her coat "Because?"

He shrugged. "I'm the boss. I need a reason?"

"C'mon, Jack. I haven't broken a glass or offended a customer."

"No, but you're not going to be cocktail waitress material for much longer. Dammit, I didn't say that," he muttered.

"But you did, so explain."

He groaned. "Pregnant women don't exactly project the right image around here," he said grudgingly.

Nikki sucked in a gulp of stale air. She needed this job almost as much as she needed to breathe. At the very least, she needed as much money as she could make before announcing her condition and seeking employment elsewhere.

"What makes you think I'm pregnant, Jack?" She tossed her coat over an empty chair and paraded herself in front of him. Thanks to the constant bouts of nausea, she still fit into her jeans. And when the waist on this pair gave, she still had the next size up before she'd have to admit defeat.

"Sorry, but it won't work. I like you, which is why I gave you a job when you had nothing to offer. I mean no experience. And you learned fast. But your..." He gnawed on the end of the cigar again, obviously uncomfortable. "Your condition makes this all wrong. Half these guys come here for the view and that won't be getting any better. Besides, if you can't drink, you shouldn't be serving drinks." He folded his arms, obviously satisfied that he'd made his point.

He hadn't.

"You still didn't answer my question. What makes you think I'm pregnant?"

"The constant trips to the bathroom... uh, you're tired..."

"Ever been married?" she asked.

"No way in hell."

"Women pee a lot, Jack. How are you feeling?"

"Been here every night this week. I'm goddamn tired. Don't change the subject."

"I've been here every night this week, too, and I'm just as tired." She braced her hands on his desk. "One more time. What makes you think I'm pregnant?"

"Look. I'm not getting involved in domestic disputes. You and your boyfriend have a problem, work it out on your own time."

Jack had just confirmed what she already knew. And when she got ahold of Kevin, she'd kill him. But first… "You know you can't discriminate. So I still have my job?"

He groaned. "As long as the boyfriend keeps his threats to himself." He grabbed for the unlit cigar again. "But only until you start to show and can't wear the uniform," he warned her.

Nikki exhaled the breath she'd been holding. "You're a prince, Jack."

"Yeah, well, just don't tell anyone."

*   *   *

Nikki pulled Janine's car up to the Victorian-style house in the suburbs. The sun shone on the gray roof and tulips had begun to bloom below the veranda. Not exactly the place she pictured Kevin Manning calling home. Too close to the white picket fence and family scene for Kevin's love 'em and leave 'em style, she thought. She wondered why he didn't just sell the old place to someone who'd appreciate its charm and potential. Family potential.

Drawing a deep breath, she banged on the door and when she got no answer, she knocked louder. Anger had propelled her this far and she needed it to keep her going. She raised her hand for one last try, and the door swung wide.

Kevin stood before her. Obviously she'd woken him. His dark hair was tousled in a sexy mess and his eyes were not yet focused. Her gaze traveled downward and she realized he wore jeans... and nothing else. Maybe he'd pulled them on before grabbing for the door because they rode low on his hips and hadn't yet been buttoned. She took in the tanned skin on his stomach and the tapered hair disappearing below his belt line and nearly lost her focus.

He cleared his throat "Nikki? What's wrong?"

Her focus returned along with her anger. "Where do you get off interfering in my life? Nearly costing me my job? My *job*." Her voice rose in pitch but she didn't care. "The one thing I need in this world if I'm going to take care of my baby."

"Our baby," he corrected her.

"And *my* responsibility. So who appointed you sole decision-maker in something that doesn't concern you?"

"Are you finished?" His sleepy-eyed gaze was gone, replaced by the determined look she knew too well.

What he didn't realize was that this time she was equally determined. "No, I'm not finished."

He reached for her hand, grasping her wrist before she could stop him. The heat of his skin caused an answering warmth to curl inside her. She fought against it, just as she planned on fighting his need to control.

His grip was gentle but remained in place. "Then let's take this inside. It's a quiet neighborhood and I wouldn't want to alienate these people before they get to know and love me." He grinned.

Nikki didn't smile back. "Lead the way," she said, not liking how those words sounded. The balance of power between them needed to shift in her favor and soon. She followed him into the house, but as soon as the door closed behind her, she yanked her arm out of his grasp.

He turned. "Come into the kitchen and we'll talk."

"Here's fine with me." She didn't see any sense in coming inside, getting comfortable, or playing nice. Not when Kevin had gone behind her back and nearly cost her her job.

"I thought we could discuss this like civilized adults. Besides, you woke me out of a deep sleep and I could use a cup of coffee." Without another word, he headed toward the kitchen.

"What would you know about civilized?" she muttered.

"I heard that. What can I get you to eat?"

Her stomach growled in response to the question. A good sign, Nikki thought, since lately just the thought of food was enough to sending her running to the nearest bathroom. Maybe the end of morning sickness was finally in sight.

She entered the now-familiar room to find Kevin standing by the fridge. "I won't be here long enough to eat. I just want to set a few ground rules."

He shrugged. "Suit yourself, but I'm starving. Talk while I make breakfast." He opened the refrigerator and she glanced over his shoulder inside. What had been pathetically empty last time she was here was now well stocked. He pulled a carton of eggs and American cheese from inside, placing them on the counter. He grabbed a bag of frozen french fries from the freezer next. "Sure I can't make you something?"

She narrowed her gaze. "Looks like you were expecting me."

He shrugged. "Let's just say I hoped."

"I *hate* games."

He met her gaze. Intense and focused eyes stared back. "And I already told you I don't play them."

"What do you call revealing my pregnancy, threatening my boss…"

"I didn't threaten. I merely explained how it would be in his best interest to see you weren't overworked." He tossed his hands in the air. "I didn't like going behind your back but you forced my hand. I couldn't stand by and watch you work yourself too hard and for no reason…"

"No reason? Try self-preservation. Or another life that's counting on me. Is that reason enough for you? Oh, I'm sorry, I forgot. You insist you'll be there for me, so maybe it never dawned on you how important it is that I rely on myself. Just in case."

Kevin narrowed his gaze, but she could see the hurt reflected there, too. She hadn't expected to feel guilty and resented the feeling that she now did.

"I realize you have no reason to trust me… but you can," he said.

"After an underhanded stunt like you pulled last night, tell me why I should."

"My father was a drunk," he said without warning. He shut the refrigerator door behind him and turned to face her head-on.

She blinked, startled at his choice of subject. "You hinted at that once."

"And my old man didn't care who supported his habit as long as there was enough booze to go around."

*   *   *

"Go on," she said, obviously confused at the relevance. But her voice had softened, which meant he'd breached her defenses.

He stepped toward her. "My parents got married right out of high school. Because they had to. My mother had no life skills, no shot at a decent job. We never knew when one of the old man's binges would start or how long one would last. Waitressing was the best she could do to bring in money."

Nikki's eyes remained locked with his. He felt curiosity and sympathy flow from her in waves. Unable to deal with the latter, Kevin figured he'd better just answer her silent questions.

"She worked because he didn't. She didn't take care of herself, didn't have the time. By the time she did get around to a doctor, it was too late."

"Kevin, I'm sorry." Her slender arms wrapped around his waist and she tipped her head back to meet his gaze.

He brushed her hair back from her face. "I couldn't handle it if something happened to you," he whispered.

"Nothing will."

He couldn't do more than try to take care of her. But with her face turned upward, her soft lips beckoning, he wanted so much more. Self-restraint came at a great cost and but he managed to get himself under control.

Until she took the initiative, pressing that welcoming mouth against his. Her lips were warm and her touch seductive. He realized she was giving comfort, but that didn't stop him from wanting, and without warning, softness turned to pure desire.

No longer tentative or hesitant, she touched her tongue to his lips and the kiss became harder, more demanding, carnal in its intensity. His hands gripped her waist and she molded her curves against him, creating unbearable friction against his already hard erection.

Kevin's grasp on sanity was tenuous at best, but he'd been tested before and he'd failed. He wasn't about to do so again. Not at Nikki's expense. Pulling back was probably the most difficult thing he'd ever done; and, seconds later, his body still demanding release, he was amazed he'd been able to do it at all.

When he managed to focus, he found Nikki's clouded eyes staring back at him. "Thank you," she muttered.

"For?"

"Calling a stop to what would have been a serious mistake."

He agreed, which was why he'd backed off first. But hearing her say it didn't sit well with him. Bruised ego or something more, he couldn't say. Or maybe he just didn't want to know.

He ran a hand through his hair. "There's too much unsettled between us to mix things up more."

Her damp lips parted as she drew a deep breath. "I agree."

He shifted positions and prayed for strength. Before he could gather his next coherent thought, she pointed to the kitchen chairs.

"Sit." Nikki slid into one of the chairs herself.

He shrugged and headed for a seat across from her, finding comfort in the barrier the old tabletop provided. "What is it?"

"Same as it was yesterday, and the day before that and the day before that. We need to reach an agreement, Kevin. One we can both live with. I need to go on with my life and you need to let me live it."

As much as he hated to admit it, she was right. Approaching her boss had been underhanded. A move borne more out of fear than rational protective instincts. He could admit that much to himself. "You want me to back off."

"That's right."

He fought an internal battle. Trusting her instincts versus trusting his own. "I still don't think the job's good for you." She opened her mouth to argue and he held up a hand to stop her. "Hear me out. You're pale, for one thing. Exhausted for another."

"And you heard the doctor. As soon as this morning sickness passes, I should be fine."

"And in the meantime?"

"I'll take it easy at work. I'll take more breaks, I promise. But you have to stop hanging around all the time. Just how are you functioning at work, anyway?"

"Not easily," he muttered. He made his own hours, already had the security in place down at the warehouse, and he wore a beeper. If he got in to work late in the morning, no one noticed. But keeping bar hours and working a day job was beginning to catch up with him.

"If you go back to living your own life, nothing will happen to me. Let's face it, Kevin. If something were to go wrong, you couldn't prevent it even if you were there."

Leave it to Nicole—perceptive, intelligent, Nicole—to figure out the crux of the problem. "Maybe not, but at least I'd be there."

This time. Did she say the words or did he merely think them?

Nikki reached out and grabbed his hand. "You can't bring Tony back by making me your number one responsibility," she said softly.

She could become much more to him than a responsibility, he thought. But she deserved better. "You're not giving me a choice, are you?"

"I can't stop you from hanging out at the bar, but I can promise to make you as miserable as possible." A grin lit the edges of her mouth and, in her eyes, he caught a glimpse of the old sparkle. She obviously sensed she'd won this round.

She had, but Kevin didn't plan to go down without a fight. "You want your freedom, you want me to back off? Then I have some conditions of my own."

SIX

O ne week without Kevin's surveillance. Nikki set a last round of drinks down onto a table filled with lingering customers. She still wasn't sure why Kevin had given in but she wasn't complaining. Although she missed his presence, missed the constant flutters in her stomach whenever he was nearby, she was also calmer knowing she was relying on herself. Of course she still had to check in with him in the mornings and again after work—but it had been her suggestion, not his. She couldn't see worrying him to distraction when a quick phone call or text would prevent it.

Nikki was working without Kevin's constant presence and she considered it a battle won.

Even better, her boss had indeed been a prince. He'd spared her cleanup duty without docking her pay. And though Nikki didn't like taking charity, she was smart enough about her situation to accept the favor.

She leaned down to stuff her tips inside her boots and without warning, doubled over in pain. Deep breaths didn't come easily, but she forced air into her lungs, hoping the cramp was one of those growing pains she'd read about and would subside. But growing pains wouldn't be in the center of her stomach, and this was.

And, damn, it hurt. Nikki leaned against the wall for support and though she'd never have believed it five minutes ago, she wished Kevin were sitting in the bar, nursing a club soda.

The smell of cigar smoke wafted in the air, and reached her nose. "Jack?" Only the wall held her upright.

"You okay? Because I'm no good around sick people. Especially sick, pregnant people."

Somehow she managed to laugh. "Don't worry. You don't have to do anything except call nine-one-one."

*   *   *

The aura of déjà vu wasn't pleasant. Kevin faced his father's landlord, the same as he'd done too many times in the past. "I'm sorry about the mess in the hall. This should more than cover cleanup costs." Kevin peeled off a hundred dollars in cash and handed it to the older man.

"But not the hassle," the landlord muttered. Privately, Kevin agreed with him. But there was no way he was paying any more for his father's drunken tantrum. Highway robbery wasn't a precedent he intended to set.

"Max'll help with the cleanup." Kevin glanced back toward the hall, wondering how he'd keep that promise. He rubbed his burning eyes. He'd rather be sleeping than taking care of his father's mess. "I'll talk to him before I leave. And thanks for calling me," Kevin said.

He headed for his father's apartment at the end of the hall. The closer he got, the more the dank smell of the old, musty building mingled with alcohol. Memories of his childhood assaulted him, none of them pleasant. Without warning, he slammed open the door to the apartment.

"What the..." His father bolted upright on the old plaid couch. Recognition dawned in Max's dark eyes, eyes that looked so much like Kevin's own—except for the added red-rimmed, bloodshot appearance.

Kevin shook his head, wishing things would change, knowing they never would. If his father hadn't sobered up when Kevin's mother had been alive, there wasn't a shot in hell he'd do it on his own.

"Hey, Kev. Nice of you to stop by. A week late for

the old birthday but what the hell. I can always use an excuse to celebrate."

Kevin stepped over a scattered pile of newspapers and an empty bag of chips. "Aren't you getting too old for this, Max?"

"Whatever happened to calling me 'Dad,' or do you think you're too old to show some respect?"

Kevin took in his father's unbuttoned jeans and stained undershirt. He closed his eyes, but he couldn't recall a time when memories of Max weren't marred by alcohol or the older man's self-pity. He couldn't remember a time when his love for his parent wasn't diluted by pain.

He faced his father once more. "Respect has to be earned," Kevin said. So did the name Dad, but Kevin wasn't up to the argument. His old man would never understand that it took more than the planting of the seed to make a man a father.

Kevin wasn't sure what to do when it came to raising his own child, but he sure as hell knew what not to do, he thought, glancing at Max.

"Sit down." His father patted the seat next to him on the couch.

Kevin shook his head. "It's late. I should be in bed. Hell, you should be in bed." He glanced at his watch. It was later than he thought. He hadn't heard from Nikki before the call from Max's landlord and he wouldn't know till he got home if she'd checked in and was okay.

He shot a disgusted glance at his father. The emergency call that brought him here had distracted him from what was really important. Or at least more immediate. Max was important; he was just a lost cause.

"I promised your landlord you'd clean up the mess in the hall. What the hell were you thinking, smashing bottles against the wall? You woke the neighbors and…"

"I didn't wake the damn neighbors, that was their mutt who wouldn't shut his mouth."

"So you figured you'd shut it for him? Ever think of picking up the phone and asking nicely?"

His father shook his head. "They don't give me any respect either," he muttered. "Damn young people think they're better than me."

Kevin rolled his eyes. For as long as he could remember, everyone thought he was better than Max Manning. "You look in the mirror lately?" He shook his head. "Never mind. You still have the janitor job in that office building downtown?"

"I'm on vacation."

"I want you to listen good. You go grovel and make sure you still have that job. I paid your rent last week. It's good through next month. After that, I expect you to make the next payment on your own."

Max rose from the couch, unsteady on his feet. "You ungrateful... think you would have made it through the academy if it wasn't for me and your mother?"

"Save the history, Max. You've got it wrong anyway." He'd give credit to his mother for anything decent he'd made of his life, but it was no thanks to his father. Another argument he refused to have.

Max took two lunging steps forward and stopped. In the old days, Kevin knew he'd have taken a swing. But no longer. Not since the day a teenage Kevin had come home to find Max beating his mother. He'd taken his father out with one punch and the old man hadn't touched him since. He never touched his wife again, either, at least not to Kevin's knowledge.

Ignoring him, Kevin headed for the kitchen and came up with a large green garbage bag. "Let's go clean up. I'll help."

His father grumbled loud and clear. Amazing, considering he'd thrown the tantrum that led to the mess. But working together, they got the hall cleared. The landlord would pocket most of Kevin's cash and maybe clean the carpet with the rest. For the sake of the other tenants, that's what Kevin hoped he'd do.

He led Max back inside. "Are you going to eat something?" Kevin asked.

"When I wake up. I need sleep."

"That makes two of us," Kevin muttered. "Remember what I said. Make sure you're gainfully employed. You do that and I'll help you out with the rent if you need it. But not if you're out of work or the money's going for booze."

They'd had the same discussion before. Inevitably, Kevin ended up bailing Max out of a jam, as he had tonight. But there wouldn't be a next time. There couldn't be. Kevin was tired of the routine and he wasn't helping his father by aiding in his addiction. Silence followed and Kevin wondered if he'd made his point. He turned back to check on Max only to find he'd passed out on the couch. Shaking his head, Kevin headed for the door.

Half an hour later, he entered his dark house and pulled his cell phone out of his pocket. Three missed calls. He turned his phone on its side and saw that it was on vibrate.

"Damn."

He checked his voicemail. Within seconds, he was back in his car and headed toward the hospital emergency room.

*   *   *

Black hair fanned against white sheets. Nikki's skin didn't hold much more color than the linen. Kevin watched through a narrow pane of glass as a nurse took Nikki's blood pressure and adjusted a belt over her abdomen. Although he told himself she was stronger than she looked, he couldn't shake the nagging fear in his gut. He tore himself away from the view and headed back to Janine in the waiting room.

Distance didn't help. His palms were sweating and his mouth felt like he'd been chewing on cotton. Kevin hadn't been this nervous since… hell, he'd never been this wound up. He ignored Janine sitting on the plastic hospital couch and paced the floor in the antiseptic waiting room.

According to Janine, Nikki had doubled over at work and the hospital had called her… when they were unable to reach Kevin, on his cell, first.

He wanted to slam his hand into the wall but refrained. It wouldn't do a damn bit of good anyhow. Sorting through his tangled feelings wasn't easy, but Kevin knew some things right off. Nikki had trusted him enough to call for him first. He should have been there when she needed him, and, absent from that, he should have been available and more on point to receive her call. Instead he was catering to his drunken father, yet again, and letting Nikki down *again* all in the span of one night's time.

Memories of the night Tony died threatened to surround him, but he shook them off, though the effort was great. Nikki needed him functioning, not wallowing in guilt.

"It wouldn't have changed anything even if you were there," Janine said.

When had he become such an easy read? "I know you mean well, but leave it alone," he muttered.

Before she responded, the doctor came through the double doors. Because the waiting room was empty, the young-looking intern didn't have to look for very long. "Are you relatives of Nicole's?" he asked.

"Yes. How is she?" Janine asked.

"She's fine. Resting more comfortably. I wouldn't call it a false alarm, but she's in no immediate danger of losing the baby."

Thank God. Kevin didn't know how many chances he'd been allotted in this lifetime, but he wasn't about to waste this one. "Can we see her?"

He nodded. "I'm going to keep her overnight for continued fetal monitoring and then if things are still status quo in the morning, she can go home." He jotted some notes down on a metal clipboard before glancing back at Kevin. "She needs to see her regular ob/gyn but, until then, there are going to be some restrictions—at least until we're certain the pregnancy will hold."

"What kind of restrictions?" Kevin asked. "And

for how long?"

"Bed rest to start. The rest is up to her primary care physician. So make sure she sees her doctor."

Kevin nodded. He didn't need to hear any more.

What came next was between him and Nikki.

*   *   *

Nikki watched the green line on the screen that monitored the baby's heartbeat and any possible contractions she might have. So far, steady and straight; no mountains signaling a potential problem.

She glanced at the beige walls and peeling paint. She hated hospitals—both their bland look and the sterile smell because they reminded her of the night Tony died. But at least she hadn't suffered another loss this time. She'd been off her feet for a few hours and the pain had begun to subside.

This whole experience seemed so surreal. Then again, the last three months had brought so many changes, she *had* entered a new world. She supposed she'd better get used to change, because on the heels of the doctor's reassurance had come his warnings and restrictions. She lay her head back against the pillow and closed her eyes, exhaustion overtaking her.

When she woke again, Kevin was sitting in a chair beside the bed, but his upper body lay forward, his head resting on the mattress beside her. She curled her fingers into the palm of her hand in an effort to resist the urge to run her hands through his hair to reassure him.

She was the one who needed reassurance, and badly. She could rely on him—Nikki knew that now. But relying on him would take her on that slippery slope toward falling in love again. And that, she couldn't allow.

He stirred and jumped up in his seat, as if realizing he'd fallen asleep on the job, she thought wryly.

He met her gaze. "At least you're smiling. I hope that means you're feeling okay."

She nodded. "Better than last night."

"You scared me to death." He met her gaze, his dark eyes shadowed from lack of sleep.

She forced a laugh. "Yeah, well, I scared myself pretty good, too. But the doctor says it's not uncommon. That not all cramping leads to..." She shook her head, unable to say the word aloud. She hadn't realized how much she wanted this baby until she thought she might lose it.

The ambulance ride to the hospital had been the scariest and loneliest few minutes of her life. And considering all that had gone on lately, Nikki knew that was saying a lot.

He grabbed her hand and held on tight. His touch was warm and reassuring on one level, and sizzling and electric on another. Seconds passed when no words were necessary. The connection between them wasn't just sexual, but basic. They were two people who shared an important bond. One, Nikki was beginning to realize, that could never be broken.

The notion scared her.

"They're discharging you this morning." Kevin shattered the silence first.

She nodded.

"You're coming home with me."

Hadn't she known that silence was golden? "I'm tired. Too tired to argue with you and that's where this is leading. So…"

"There are no arguments, Nicole. Just plain hard facts." He held up one finger. "Fact one. You're pregnant and have been restricted to bed rest. Total and complete bed rest until the first trimester's over."

She'd argue if she could, but so far Kevin hadn't said anything inaccurate. It was just his solutions she found fault with and he hadn't mentioned those again. Yet. She folded her arms over her chest. "Go on."

"So who's going to fix your meals? Do your shopping? Be around in case there's a problem? Janine? I don't think that's fair, expecting her to handle two pregnancies, do you? Besides, she's leaving at the end of the week. She wanted to cancel her flight, but I insisted you'd be well taken care of."

Nikki shut her eyes. Not only was he persistent, but he was also right She couldn't be a burden to Janine. She'd never even consider it. But why had fate doomed her to be someone's responsibility, especially Kevin's? Why, when she was just getting her life together, did she have to end up flat on her back? Her savings were minimal, but if she could have hung on for another few months of work…

"You aren't exactly in a position to babysit," she reminded him. "Don't you have to work?"

"I've given this a lot of thought. Don hired me to put a new security system in place and screen employees. The system's been up and working for a while now. I need to do check-ins and updates, but I don't need to work nine to five. And I can hire a housekeeper for the hours I'm out of the house."

The room began to spin and Nikki grabbed onto the bedrail. "You do not have to plan your entire life around me. I'm perfectly capable of staying alone during the day."

"Not in a walk-up apartment, so you can forget that idea now. Can we at least agree Janine's place isn't going to work?"

The thought of three flights of stairs was overwhelming now and she felt her options closing in on her. "Yes," she admitted. "Janine's place is out. So say I move in…" She swallowed over the lump and forced the next words from her throat. "With you?" God, how would she survive living with Kevin on a day-to-day basis? Knowing he was taking care of her because she was carrying his child? Dealing with the constant sexual awareness he generated inside her? Coping with the knowledge she cared too much about the loner ex-cop?

She shook her head and continued, "Say I move in with you? There's no reason you have to spend money on a housekeeper just to look out for me."

He shrugged. "I was going to hire someone anyway."

"Once a week, maybe. But daily…"

"Damn it, Nicole, do you really have to argue every little point? Look around you. What are your options? I know I'm no prince, but I'm the best you've got so make the best of it, okay?" He ran a frustrated hand through his hair, and Nikki suffered a rush of shame.

She didn't want to be a burden or an obligation, but she couldn't change the fact that she was. Kevin would view her that way whether she liked it or not. She might not like it, but she was damn lucky she had Kevin willing to take her in. "I appreciate all you want to do for me. And yes, I'll move in. Thank you."

"You're welcome."

"But I'm not giving in on the full-time maid, so

you can forget that now."

*   *   *

Kevin stifled a groan. The last thing he wanted was to upset her. He respected her independence, much as she thought otherwise. To have her grovel didn't please him or do anything for his male ego.

He'd won his most important concession. She was moving in. No need to push further. "Okay. Part-time help it is," he said.

She raised her eyebrows. "That was almost too easy."

"Disappointed?" he asked.

She smiled. "No. Just relieved."

"Good." Apparently he'd made another point then. He wouldn't abandon her or his child. Did she believe him? He shook his head, knowing he didn't want to delve deeply into the answer.

"Okay then. I'll go over to Janine's and pack up your things before coming back for you."

She nodded.

The conversation hadn't gone as smoothly as he'd hoped, and now wasn't the time to bring up her other problems. The baby would be covered under his insurance, but Nikki would not. She had no coverage for any medical bills or serious problems that might yet arise. Nor did she have the money to cover the bills for the medical care both she and the baby deserved right now.

Although he'd been impressed by the clinic and its range of services, the distance between his suburban home and the city clinic wasn't safe, should there be another emergency. Add to that the location, which made him uneasy in the first place, and Kevin thought he had a good argument for switching to a private doctor in a suburban hospital. Not that Nikki would agree.

If he could get past her pride, there was much he could offer, including paying for her pregnancy medical care—like the emergency room visit last night. The solution he had in mind, however, would probably scare the living daylights out of her, because it sure as hell rocked his world.

Marriage. Commitment. Trust. He shuddered, knowing how he ranked in that particular department. Although he'd pay for Nikki's care regardless of whether she became his wife or not, the baby needed the legalities of marriage. Because then his child would have his name. And so would Nikki, from there on in. No illegitimate stigma, no complications.

He glanced over. Her eyes were still moist, her jaw clamped tight. She'd given in, but not willingly. He was the last person she wanted to turn to for anything. He didn't blame her, but she had no choice. So, yes, he'd won one battle, but he had a hunch that was nothing compared to the fight ahead.

*　　*　　*

Nikki stepped inside the front door and glanced around Kevin's new house as if seeing it for the first time. And in a way she was. For the foreseeable future, this was her new home. Her stomach cramped and it had nothing to do with the baby. Directly in front of her was a large staircase leading to the second floor of his Victorian-style home.

"Consider the upstairs off-limits," Kevin said, coming up behind her.

"Believe me, I wouldn't dream of going near those steps," she muttered.

"Good. I just wanted to make sure we were in agreement." He stood so close, his warm breath tickled her neck, sending a shot of awareness throughout her body.

Whenever she was around Kevin, she burned. Nikki hoped he kept a fire extinguisher somewhere close because she had a hunch she was going to need it. She took a step forward but she still felt his solid presence behind her.

"So where's my room?" she asked lightly, trying to minimize her feelings about setting up house with Kevin.

"Back here. Apparently this old place had a serv-ants' quarters off the kitchen. There's a bedroom and full bath."

"Good. Good." With his bedroom upstairs, she was half a house and a full flight of stairs away from temptation.

He stepped around her, motioning for her to fol-low. With the soft denim molding to his thighs and the ripple of muscles beneath his old gray T-shirt Nikki would have followed him to the ends of the earth. And back.

She swallowed a moan. Boy was she in trouble.

He stopped in the family room, in front of what looked like a brand-new leather recliner. "I figured you wouldn't want to be cooped up in a back room all day, so you can make yourself comfortable in here."

Sunlight streamed through oblong windows around the perimeter of the room, making for a welcoming place to be. A stack of women's magazines sat on the table beside the chair, and a large-screen television was directly in front. "This is... this is perfect Kevin, thank you."

He shifted from foot to foot, obviously uncom-fortable with her gratitude. "I stopped at the hospital gift shop," he said, pointing to the neat pile of reading he'd left for her.

"Thanks." If this stiltedness continued, the stress

would send her right back to the hospital.

"I did a quick pack-and-run when I was in your apartment earlier. Janine said she'd come by this afternoon to visit and help you get your things put away. I didn't think you'd want me to unpack for you." His cheekbones were highlighted with color—embarrassment—making him appear endearing and… soft. A word and a look she'd never associated with Kevin before.

But with this offer and unexpected move into his home, she was seeing a fresh side to Kevin Manning. She had a hunch they'd be seeing new and enlightening sides to each other, for as long as this arrangement continued.

"I have to let my boss know I'm out of commission," Nikki said, thinking of all the repercussions.

"At the risk of starting an argument, I took a chance and called over there this morning. I spoke to Jack myself. I figured you'd want to give him as much notice as possible, all things considered."

Her gaze met his. No doubt he expected another argument. "That was thoughtful. Thank you."

"You're welcome. I'm going to make a few calls. The remote's on the table."

"I'll be fine."

"You should get off your feet."

She nodded and lowered herself into the comfortable chair. The leather squeaked as it molded to the contours of her body. She pushed herself back into a reclining position. Tension in her back and legs—tension she hadn't even known she was carrying, eased immediately. She sighed aloud. "This is great."

"And you know where the bathroom is."

"I'm not likely to forget." She laughed and he grinned in return. The unbearable tension between them had finally been broken. Nikki wondered how long the reprieve would last.

SEVEN

"I hate being waited on." Nikki tilted her head back and watched as the woman Kevin had hired, Eleanor Reid, cleaned off the dinner table while she did nothing but sit.

"I'm just doing my job," Eleanor reminded her. A job she'd done well in the last week. Problem was, the job was all she did. There was no small talk or chit-chat.

Nikki figured she could either lose her mind or try to draw the older woman out. "Yeah, but I grew up on a farm. Everyone pitched in. I mean even the cows gave milk."

It worked. The other woman cracked a smile on her professional face. Nikki waved a hand toward one of the chairs, motioning for her to sit.

Eleanor hesitated, then sat down beside Nikki at the table. "How are you feeling?" she asked finally.

After three days a week of Mrs. Reid puttering around her but never invading her personal space, Nikki was grateful she'd penetrated her shell. Nikki was lonely.

Funny, but even in college, she'd been independent. She had many friends, and a roommate, but she'd been on her own more often than not. And after Tony died, she and Janine had lived opposite schedules, which left Nikki alone during the day. She hadn't been lonely then.

But she was now. Because for the first time she knew what it was like to live with someone—and be totally, utterly alone. Oh, Kevin was around, her constant companion when not at work, making sure she felt okay, didn't get out of bed too often and wanted for nothing. But he was as distant as he could be with the constant awareness sizzling between them.

Perhaps because of her strong feelings for him, Nikki felt the emptiness that much more. Which made her determined not to take this confinement lying down. She had to approach the future as if it didn't involve Kevin, and prepare both herself and her baby for that eventuality.

But she smiled at her companion. "I'm feeling okay."

"Good, because some women would be climbing the walls after a week of bed rest."

Nikki dropped her head to her hands, which lay on the table. "I lied. I'm not okay. I'm bored out of my mind," she wailed. She lifted her head and grinned. "Thank you. I feel much better now."

"When are you due?"

Her hand went to her stomach, as it automatically did each time she thought of the baby. "Early November."

"A Scorpio. Determined little buggers with long memories. Protective of those they care about."

"Sounds a lot like his father," Nikki murmured. She'd begun thinking of the baby in terms of *he*, probably because she envisioned a tough little guy like Kevin.

"Mmm. Baby's lucky to have such a caring man as a parent. Not all kids get that lucky."

She wondered if Kevin thought of his son—or daughter—as lucky to have him for a father. Though she hadn't planned this pregnancy, she knew *she* thought her baby was fortunate to have him around. But he'd been on a downward spiral of guilt since Tony died. If nothing else, maybe this baby would give him a positive focus.

"You're perceptive, Mrs…. Can I call you Eleanor? I mean if we're going to be cooped up together, the formality seems kind of silly, doesn't it?"

"Eleanor it is." She smiled in return. "You seem

perceptive yourself, for one so young."

Nikki shrugged. "Let's say I've lived a lot in a short time."

"Well, you and Mr. Manning seem like a nice young couple."

They were nice, and young... but a couple? Nikki shook her head, knowing if Kevin had his way, "they" would never be an "us."

Did he realize what the future *could* hold? What kind of family life the three of them could have, *if he opened his heart?* Shivering at the direction of her thoughts, she sought for a way to change the subject.

Eleanor did it for her. She cleared her throat. "I really should clean this mess up, though, before Mr. Manning gets home."

Nikki nodded. But she dreaded the thought of another long evening. "If you finish early... would you be interested in a game of cards?" Nikki asked. Kevin had left her a deck earlier. For Solitaire. She grimaced.

"I'm not much of a card player, but I did see a Scrabble board on the top shelf of the closet when I was cleaning."

Nikki's brain kicked into gear for the first time in four months. Waitressing was good for her checkbook, but the mental stimulation had been minimal. Unless she counted the numerous ways of ducking a come-on, she thought wryly. "That sounds great."

"Why don't you rest for awhile and I'll come get you when I'm finished in here."

Nikki nodded. She yawned, amazed she could be tired when all she did was lounge around. With Kevin due home soon, and with him, the return of tension, she might as well gather her strength while she could.

Once in her room, she lay down on the gingham checked comforter and stretched until she found a comfortable position. Her gaze fell to a small bouquet of freshly cut flowers in a vase on the dresser. A gift from Janine, they reminded her of many things. Especially the life growing inside her and the dream that she'd one day have the family she'd always wanted. She couldn't base her future on hope.

She pulled open her dresser drawer and withdrew her college transcripts and deferral letter. Though she'd always wanted to be a stay-at-home mother, she'd wanted to make the choice, not be forced into it out of necessity. The only way she'd have all her options open to her was if she finished her last semester of student teaching and graduated college.

With or without Kevin—whether he liked it or not—she had to get her degree and reestablish her independence. Or she'd lose herself and all the progress she'd made.

* * *

Kevin checked the locks on the warehouse door and headed back inside. The security cameras he'd installed would monitor comings and goings in detail, and so would the guard stationed at the desk. As a result, not only were his hands free, but so was his mind. Free to focus on Nikki and what he'd come to think of as the invasion of his home.

Having always lived alone, he'd grown used to complete silence. Not that he'd liked it, but it was all he'd known. And it was preferable to the sound of a drunk knocking into furniture or the constant fighting he'd grown up with.

When he'd moved into the old house, he hadn't bothered with any kind of decorating beyond what his aunt had done—though with a baby on the way, he'd have to give some sort of thought to change. But for now, he had his hands full with his female... What did he call her?

Houseguest was too generic a term for the soft female lounging in oversized tops and looking far too warm and welcoming for his peace of mind. He'd managed to keep his distance so far, but it hadn't been easy. It took every ounce of discipline he'd learned on the force not to gather her into his arms and keep her there.

A dangerous notion. He'd be a fool if he didn't see the matching longing in her violet eyes, or acknowledge the emotional connection between them. But to act on either would be to put his needs first, not Nikki's. He'd done that once before, with disastrous results.

Not disastrous for him, since the thought of her pregnant with his child was a blessing. One he didn't deserve. And one that had uprooted her entire life. Again. With his track record of letting her down, he didn't intend to take any chances. So he intended to keep his distance and put *her* first for once. And maybe then he could look himself in the mirror without wanting to hit the reflection staring back at him.

By the time he walked back into the house, Mrs. Reid had finished cleaning up, had set his wrapped dinner on the counter and was ready to leave for the night. He glanced over the woman's shoulder, expecting to see Nikki settled in the recliner watching television, but the room was sparkling clean—and empty.

"Where's Nikki?" he asked.

"In bed. Asleep."

"Is she feeling okay?" Their trip to the clinic earlier in the week had been uneventful and the recommendation of the doctor was not much different than that of the emergency room attendant in the hospital.

Kevin wanted to broach the subject of leaving the clinic, but he didn't think Nikki was up to the argument. And he was certain she'd fight him. On this, as well as other things. Kevin knew he had to build the foundation for approaching the subject of marriage in a way that would leave Nikki with no doubt it was the right solution. He just hadn't yet figured out how to make his case.

Mrs. Reid grabbed for her light jacket and swung it over her shoulders. "She's fine. I don't even think it's real exhaustion. She's bored if you ask me. Had it with being cooped up."

He exhaled. "Can't say I blame her, but it shouldn't be too much longer." Another week and she'd return to the doctor, and if things stayed the same, she'd be allowed out of bed as long as she didn't do anything strenuous.

"Boredom often comes from loneliness," Mrs. Reid said with a pointed stare. "Can I speak my mind?"

Kevin nodded. Some insight into Nikki wouldn't only help her, but it might make this new living arrangement more bearable. "Go on."

"I didn't realize, until tonight, that she wanted me to do more than clean around her and serve her meals. She wants company. Someone to talk to and some plain human interaction. We all need it."

"Are you asking my permission to spend time with her? Even though you're only here part-time, I hired you to be with her for whatever she needs. Not just to cook and clean."

She shook her head. He thought she muttered, "Men," under her breath. "Of course I'll keep that girl company. I like her spirit. But I'm not the only one she needs something from." She fished for her keys in her black leather purse. "Good night, Mr. Manning."

"Night," he muttered, knowing she was right. And not knowing what the hell to do about it.

He let Mrs. Reid out. Following instinct, he made his way toward Nikki's room. She'd left the hall light burning but her room was dark. Kevin walked down the brightly lit hall toward the door, open just a crack. With any other woman, he'd consider it an invitation. But Nikki had never resorted to playing games.

Even the night she'd shown up on his doorstep, she hadn't been shy about what she wanted. He stepped into the room, his gaze drawn to the figure in the bed. He walked closer. Her even breathing told him she was asleep.

He ought to turn and go. He'd done his duty. He'd checked and she was fine. He could leave her in peace. Yet he couldn't bring himself to walk out. Instead he sat beside her on the double bed, careful not to move the mattress and wake her up. As if of its own volition, his hand moved, and he smoothed the dark hair off her forehead.

She stirred, rolling toward him. So much for good intentions, he thought.

"Kevin?" she murmured, her voice groggy with sleep.

"Right here."

Her eyes opened slowly, and her gaze met his. Surprise warred with pleasure. Pleasure she quickly stifled and he felt its loss. "What's wrong?" she asked.

"Just wanted to make sure you were okay." It was too late to remove his hand, nor did he want to. He'd spent too much time keeping them apart but wanting more. He fingered the silken strands between his fingers.

He'd believed the only way their new living arrangement could work was if he kept his distance. He still believed that, but knew it was the selfish man's way out. "So are you okay?" he asked.

* * *

Nikki bit down on her lower lip. She held onto Kevin's gaze and decided, if she had any hope of happiness, that she had to be honest. "I'm fine," she told him. "Better, now that you're here."

His sharp inhale told her she'd hit a nerve. Well, good. It's about time someone didn't let Kevin off easily. All this tiptoeing around each other wasn't good for her and wasn't good for the baby. If she wasn't careful she'd end up in a self-induced depression and there was no way she'd let these circumstances get her down. It meant pulling Kevin into the feeling world, kicking and screaming, but she didn't care.

If she was going to live in his house and be around him constantly, then he was going to have to acknowledge that he wasn't alone. That she was here, and she affected him as much as he affected her. Not that she expected anything more to come of it, she assured herself.

Perhaps this nap gave her more strength and perspective than she'd realized. Or maybe it was breaking through Mrs. Reid's reserve, but something had changed. She was pregnant, she was happy about it, and she wasn't going to let confinement get to her. She was going to live, and drag Kevin along with her.

"I can't stay."

She pushed herself higher against the pillows. "Why? Do you have important reruns to watch on television? Push-ups to do that can't wait?"

A grin edged the sides of his mouth. "You aren't going to make this easy on me, are you?"

"Why should I? I'm living in your house and having your baby. What about this is easy for me?"

"You're too smart for your own good, Nicole."

She laughed. "No, just too stubborn for yours. Stay with me," she said, knowing she'd be catching him off guard. "Please." She added the latter for good measure.

He leaned forward and studied her with his intense, dark-eyed gaze. She caught a whiff of his masculine scent and her insides curled with a rush of pleasure. By asking him to stay, she realized she was torturing herself with what she couldn't have, and yet she wanted nothing more than to wake up with Kevin beside her.

"Mrs. Reid says you're lonely."

"It's a combination of things. Boredom is one of them, but she's right. I'm lonely. In here." She tapped on her chest right above her heart. "It's hard to explain. Maybe some of it's hormonal, what with the baby and all—but…"

He narrowed his eyes as she spoke, absorbing every word. "Go on."

"We created this life together. But when I found out I was pregnant, I didn't want to burden you. I planned on doing this on my own, but you pushed and pushed until you became a part of things. And now… here I am. But we're further apart than ever."

He let out a groan. "You know what I am, what I'm capable of. Isn't it better if we just…"

"Shut up and lie down, will you?" She patted the bed beside her. Nikki wasn't in the mood to hear how they were better off operating separately, how she shouldn't put her faith in him because he'd let her down. She was tired of the argument, tired of the knowledge, and all she wanted was his shoulder to lean on for just one night.

With an unexpected chuckle, he eased himself beside her. The double bed dipped beneath his weight and the sudden rush of warmth and pleasure blindsided her.

"You're a bossy female, you know that?" he asked.

"I suppose there are worse things I could be."

He held out an arm and she curled into him, with an ease and a sense of rightness that shook her very soul. Because she could so easily get used to this. To him.

And he could just as easily take it all away.

*   *   *

Kevin woke up with Nikki curled in his arms. He didn't remember falling asleep and he didn't remember ever sleeping so soundly. Then again, he'd never spent the *entire* night with Nikki.

That first time he'd woken with a jolt, realized what he'd done and bolted like a coward. Well, no more. It was past time he faced what he'd done, accept responsibility and go from there. His arms encircled her waist and his palms lay against her stomach. Though still flat, within weeks, a slight bulge would rise. His child.

"Can you feel a difference?" The sleepy murmur caught him off guard.

"Not yet."

"He's in there."

"He?"

She shrugged. "I guess I've got a gut feeling."

A son. "Do you have a preference?" he asked.

"Mmm-hmm. Healthy. You?"

"The same." He inhaled and caught the scent of her hair.

He didn't miss the intimacy of the situation, or the fact that each moment like this drew him further from his solitary way of living. Drew him closer to Nikki.

"We created a life," she murmured.

He wanted to relive those memories and his hand, involuntarily, molded against her soft flesh as he remembered the night in vivid detail and the mood changed from intimate to sexually charged. His fingertips dipped lower and hit a wide band of lace. He paused, and when she didn't stop him or object, he slipped his fingers lower, beneath the scalloped edging.

Her sharp intake of air gave him pause. But only for an instant. Because she wrapped her hand around his wrist and urged him on. There was a part of him that knew better, and a part of him that responded to her silent plea. Not just his body reacted to the knowledge that she still wanted him. Something inside him, that had been cold for so long, began to thaw.

She made him feel in so many different ways. He wanted her. On many different levels. It wasn't because he'd been celibate since Nikki—although he had. And it wasn't because she was any willing female. She was Nikki and she was special.

She always had been. And now she was carrying his child, he thought almost reverently. The reminder should have made him want to pull back, but the craving for her overruled his brain. And besides, she couldn't... complete the act, as per doctor's orders. Just recalling that conversation, and her bright red flush, made him grin.

"It's not like you to be a tease," she whispered.

"Ever hear of building anticipation?" he asked. His fingertips brushed over her heated skin and the sensitive mound beneath.

She sucked in a heavy breath and her hips bucked toward his hand, as if searching for more of his touch.

"Like that, Princess?" he asked, making sure the tip of his finger met with that one sensitive spot.

Her answer was a breathy moan. One that sent him reeling and caused his body to harden in anticipation. Anticipation of nothing, he reminded himself, but certain body parts didn't seem to care.

Without warning, she turned to face him. Dark

strands of hair brushed her cheeks, and her eyes were wide in her makeup-free face. "I think you're playing with fire."

∗   ∗   ∗

He touched her cheek. "Why's that?"

"For a number of reasons, but let's start with the fact that we can't finish this." Nikki wasn't about to mention the fact that with a simple touch, not only did he make her burn, but he made her care again. She hadn't stopped, but at least she'd been able to lie to herself. It wouldn't be as easy from here on in. "We can't…"

"Yes, we can." His intense gaze told her she wasn't off the hook. "There are many ways to…" He broke off without finishing the sentence.

"Make love, Kevin." She finished it for him. Otherwise she'd probably have to hear the male version of what they'd been about to do. Sex was as far from what she'd be doing with Kevin as the sun was from the moon. "But don't worry. You don't have to say the words since we aren't about to do anything anyway."

His face paled. "Why turn this into an argument over semantics?" He reached out to touch her.

It was all she could do not to roll into a protective ball. "Because those *semantics* mean a lot to me. But that aside, the doctor said there's to be no penetration or orgasm until further notice." Though she couldn't meet his gaze, she forced herself to be as clinical about things as the doctor had been.

It was an uncomfortable and embarrassing topic, but she'd rather discuss what they couldn't do as opposed to what Kevin *didn't* feel. "Semantics," she mimicked under her breath.

He rolled over, his arm covering his eyes. "I'd like to say I'm sorry I started this."

"But you're not."

He exhaled a groan. "Of course I am. But not for the reasons you think. And if I say it shouldn't have happened, you'll take it the wrong way and jump all over me."

"Just spit it out. What is it you're trying to say?" she asked, then steeled herself for what was to come.

"There's something between us. It's sexual…"

"Tell me something I don't know," she muttered.

"And it's emotional."

"And it's the emotional that makes you run like hell."

He raised himself up onto one side. When she continued staring at the ceiling, he grabbed for her chin and turned her head to face him. Looking into his eyes was painful, but nothing she hadn't experienced before, she thought sadly. "It's not the emotional that makes me run. It's you."

"Talk clearly," she said, frustration pouring through her. "I don't get you, and God help me, I want to."

"Everything you are, everything you offer me is good—and I don't deserve it. Hell, I can't live up to it. I can't give you what you want, what you need. And every time I look into your eyes, I realize that."

"Guilt again. You think you're responsible for Tony. That you let me down."

He clenched his jaw tight. "I did."

"Yeah, you did. And I expected too much from one night. We're past that."

His humorless laugh chilled her. "Way past. And in too deep."

She shut her eyes, knowing arguing with him now would be like driving in a never-ending circle. She'd never get anywhere. He carried too much guilt to ever forgive himself and he viewed her as some sort of paragon of virtue that he'd never be worthy of.

He didn't see himself for the good and decent man he was any more than he viewed her as an ordinary person with flaws, someone who also made mistakes. With his two skewed perceptions of reality, she doubted they'd ever be able to meet in the mortal world.

"Okay, Kevin. You win." She ignored her tingling breasts and the heaviness between her legs. Sex was easy. Her relationship with Kevin was not. "I'd rather be lonely than tortured."

"Oh, hell."

"I couldn't have said it better myself," Nikki said.

EIGHT

Nikki glanced around Janine's bedroom. What was once her brother's bedroom, she thought sadly. Unfortunately, not much had changed in the few months since Tony's death.

His side of the bed still had his things on the nightstand. A copy of *Sports Illustrated* lay beside a small clock, his watch sat beside it, and the hardcover mystery novel Nikki had bought him for his birthday, a few weeks before he died, was propped against a bedside lamp.

She turned to the closet where Janine was inside choosing clothes for her week's trip to Iowa. Tony's uniforms and casual clothes still hung on one side of the large walk-in closet. She recalled the day he'd decided to rent this place, and jokingly said it was the only apartment in town with a closet large enough to keep his new wife from stealing valuable clothing space. Nikki grinned. Tony had been joking, of course. Neither he nor Janine were into shopping or acquiring huge wardrobes—no more than they were into arguing over whose space was whose.

With a sigh, she lowered herself onto a small chair in the corner of the room. Janine was right to leave. The memories here were overwhelming. The move would force her to pack away the past and move on with the present in a way she probably couldn't handle otherwise. Because she'd been so in love with Tony.

Nikki glanced at the ceiling, blinking through the moisture that filled her eyes. Janine and her brother had made the most of their time together. How many couples could claim the same?

How many couples were given the opportunity?

A chill shook her, as she realized the direction her thoughts were taking. She and Kevin were being given that same chance. Maybe they weren't in *love*—or at least he wasn't. She, on the other hand, could topple with the slightest bit of encouragement. Perhaps she was already there. Always had been. But now they were bound together by an unborn life, a baby that would need them forever. *Them.*

She was already living in his house. Physically, they were drawn together. Emotionally, they both held back. Only a concerted effort on one of their parts kept them from finding what Janine and Tony had shared.

Or was she deluding herself, Nikki wondered. Wanting to believe in unicorns when no such creature existed? She would never know unless she went looking. Unless she made the effort to create a warm, family atmosphere in the house she now called home.

A new resolve took hold. She'd take dual roads. On the one hand, she'd prepare herself for *the end*, should it come. But in the meantime, she would give it her best shot. And hope Kevin didn't shoot her down and destroy what few dreams remained in her heart.

Janine walked out of the closet, a pile of clothes on hangers in her arms. "I'm still uncomfortable leaving you," she said as she dumped the heavy load onto the bed beside an open suitcase.

Nikki nodded. "I know you are. And a week ago I'd have told you to go and assured you I'd be fine." She bit down on her lower lip, realizing how her attitude had changed in the five minutes since she'd walked into this room. "I'd have been lying then."

Janine paused from her task of unhooking the clothes from the hangers and refolding them to fit into the one piece of luggage. "And now?"

Nikki shrugged. "Let's just say I've had an epiphany." She wrapped her arms around her bent legs and smiled. "I'm trying to see beyond that tunnel vision you accused me of having. I'm going to try to make things work with Kevin."

Janine's eyes widened in surprise. "Why the change of heart?"

Her heart hadn't changed its beat. She'd just accepted what she'd always known deep inside. Her feelings for Kevin ran deep. If she wanted the life she'd always craved, she had to take a risk and hold onto the opportunity that presented itself now.

Nikki let her gaze take in the bedroom once more. "Life is short. I don't want to miss out on what could have been because I was too stubborn to see what was right in front of me." Too scared to trust in Kevin again.

Her sister-in-law crossed the room and grabbed Nikki's hand. "For what it's worth, I think you're doing the right thing. It's what *I* would do if I were you."

"But?" Nikki sensed the hesitation in Janine's tone.

"As much as I wanted you to open your mind and give Kevin a chance, we both know it's a risk."

She nodded. "I'll prepare for that just in case. I may never break through that reserve or the doubts he lives with." Though she planned to try.

The childhood—and alcoholic father—he rarely mentioned had left him with scars and the sense that he deserved the solitary life he'd created. If his past had formed the man he'd become, Nikki hoped to help reshape his future.

"Wish me luck, Janine." Because she had the distinct sense she would need it.

*   *   *

To Nikki's chagrin, Kevin had made himself scarce over the weekend. She'd left him alone, giving him his last hours of peace and solitude, she thought wryly. Her Friday afternoon doctor's appointment had been rescheduled for Monday. The shuffle had given Kevin an excuse to hole up in the basement to clean and box some of his aunt's things.

Nikki didn't mind. Before she put any sort of plan into action, she wanted the doctor's permission to get back on her feet. So here she was, sitting beside Kevin in the small office at Planned Parenthood, waiting for the okay that would shift both their lives.

Silence surrounded them, but again, Nikki let him have his way. A false sense of security, she thought, but he didn't know that. Yet.

A brief knock sounded and the door swung open wide. Dr. Molloy breezed into the room, a smile on her face. "I'm glad to see you two here together."

Nikki had been through the examination on her own, but Kevin wanted to be present for the discussion. Not only was Nikki grateful for his interest, she also wouldn't turn down the chance at shared intimacy.

He reached over and grabbed for Nikki's hand, taking her by surprise. "We're in this together. Nikki understands that now."

A rush of pleasure curled inside her stomach. Careful, she warned herself. She could not allow herself to mistake Kevin's concern over the baby for caring about *her*. She'd have to cultivate those emotions every chance she got, while somehow protecting herself from more pain.

The physician nodded. "Admirable. Too many couples let an unexpected pregnancy drive them apart. But you two seem levelheaded and secure in your relationship now." She was obviously referring to their first run-in at the clinic—one Nikki would prefer to forget. "I'm glad," the doctor said.

Kevin squeezed her hand. An overt show of support, certainly. An agreement with the doctor? Possibly. Their night together, earlier in the week, had reinforced the truth: Kevin wasn't ready to consider a relationship between them.

"So what's the verdict?" he asked.

Dr. Molloy glanced down at the paperwork on her cluttered desk. "The exam was fine, no problems for the last two weeks. You're ending your first trimester. I don't see any reason why you can't get back on your feet as long as you take care of yourself. Frequent rests and don't overdo it. No waitressing," she said pointedly.

"I think Nicole and I have already reached an understanding there."

Nikki ignored his attempt at asserting control. "I wouldn't do anything to jeopardize the pregnancy," she assured the doctor, whom she'd come to trust.

With a smile, Dr. Molloy closed the manila folder she'd scribbled her notes into. "Any other questions?"

"What's the policy on…" Kevin cleared his throat. "What I meant to say was, how would you feel about us…" Nikki looked at him, waiting to hear his question.

"You can resume sexual relations any time, no restrictions—except nothing too strenuous," Dr. Molloy warned them.

The answer was so unexpected, Nikki nearly choked on her own saliva. She coughed and Kevin grabbed her arm. "Are you okay?"

She was fine—she hoped. In all her hopes for the future, she'd forced herself to forget the possibilities of making love with Kevin. But once the doctor put the notion out there, Nikki couldn't help thinking about how solid and secure she'd felt in his arms or about the waves of pleasure he was capable of giving.

She wrapped her arms around her chest, as if the small gesture could ward off the sexual awakening.

With difficulty, she turned and met his gaze. His cheekbones were flushed with color. At least he'd thrown himself into turmoil, too. "Did you get the correct answer?" she asked.

"No, but I like the one I got," he murmured, soft enough for only her to hear. His voice was a low growl and her insides turned to mush with a rush of desire.

"I'm sorry. Did I misinterpret the question?" Dr. Molloy asked.

Kevin shifted in his seat. "Actually, yes. My concern was very different."

Some kind of internal radar went off in Nikki's brain. She couldn't put her finger on the reason, but Kevin's flat tone made her wary. So did his sudden shift in body language. Stiff posture, squared shoulders, and clenched jaw. Nikki was certain neither she nor the doctor would like what was to come.

Dr. Molloy clasped her hands and leaned forward in her seat. Did she sense an upcoming problem, too? "What can I do for you, Mr. Manning?"

He leaned forward in his seat. "It's not that I'm questioning your qualifications or abilities."

"But?"

Nikki shut her eyes, now realizing where he was headed. "Kevin," she said, clear warning in her tone. Her choice in doctors was a topic they could discuss in private.

The doctor waved her hand. "Let him speak. He's entitled to his opinion."

"However wrong it may be," Nikki muttered.

"I haven't voiced one yet," he said. "Look, forgive me for any inherent bias, but we're in a clinic in an area far from where Nikki now lives. As far as I can tell, she's got a risky pregnancy."

"Actually, she doesn't. What Ms. Welles had is perfectly common among pregnant women. We restrict their activity as a precaution and to avoid miscarriage. Though there are schools of thought that say if a miscarriage was going to occur, bed rest couldn't stop it."

"Regardless, there's another school of thought that adheres to the expression *the best money can buy*. It's not that I question your abilities, but I wonder whether a private doctor would…"

"Charge a higher price that I can't afford, for one thing." Nikki rose from her seat and turned to face him. "Are you nuts? I thought we agreed to let me live my own life. And here you are, questioning my choices in front of my doctor. Gee, that shows a lot of faith."

"I believe I said I *wondered* whether a private doctor couldn't offer you more. I was asking Dr. Molloy's opinion, not questioning your choices. You made an excellent decision to come here. Under the circumstances," Kevin said.

"Excuse me." Dr. Molloy cleared her throat, "Didn't I mention that stress isn't good for mother or child?"

With a loud exhale for exaggerated effect, Nikki lowered herself back into her seat. Just when she'd decided to try to build a relationship, he placed unexpected roadblocks in her path.

"The most I can do is offer you some pros and cons and suggest the two of you talk this over, rationally, at home."

Kevin nodded. Nikki tensed. Why discuss anything, when she sensed she'd be outvoted? "I'd like to hear what you have to say," she said to the doctor.

*   *   *

Good, Kevin thought. But he wasn't fooled. Nikki wasn't at all interested in the doctor's opinion, just in throttling him. He'd made another calculated error when it came to dealing with Nicole. He should have discussed the possibility of switching doctors with her in private. Instead he'd put her on the defensive.

He hadn't meant to. Rather, he figured that laying out his case in front of a third party would be beneficial to them both. When would he learn? He had little experience dealing with women's emotions. Especially pregnant women. Trial by fire, he thought, catching sight of her clenched jaw and firm expression.

She didn't seem to mind his questions or concerns, but she took affront any time he tried to wrest control. Control and independence she'd worked hard to achieve. Dammit, he hadn't meant to take that away from her.

"Let's lay out the facts," the doctor suggested.

He nodded. It was why he'd broached the subject to begin with.

"Fact one. You picked this clinic when you lived closer. Fact two. We're open limited hours. Fact three. I volunteer here, but my main base is outside of the city." Dr. Molloy grinned. "This might help you two split the difference." She reached into her jacket pocket and handed Nikki a business card.

Nikki turned the card over in her hand. "This hospital is close to Kevin's house."

"You'd get to keep your doctor, and he'd get his private physician."

"But someone would have to pay you your out of clinic fees," she said.

The doctor rose to her feet. Kevin followed. "And that's my cue. The rest has to be worked out between the two of you."

When she shut the door behind her, Kevin heard the silence. He turned to face Nikki, but she'd slipped around him and before he could blink, she disappeared out the door.

*   *   *

The wind blew her hair off her face. Nikki tipped her chin up to catch the wind and feel its cool relief. *He doesn't want to control; he wants to protect.*

Reminding herself about Kevin's motives helped to calm down her anger, but it didn't change the fact that he'd circled around her in the hopes of getting his way. Some start to reaching an accommodation, she thought with frustration.

He caught up with her outside the clinic. "At the very least, let me drive you home."

"I wasn't running away from you. I needed fresh air."

"Space from me."

She sighed. "I'd think that was obvious."

He gently took her elbow and steered her toward the end of the street, toward his car, which he'd parked on the next block. He opened the door, then walked around to the driver's side. Minutes later, they were on their way.

"I can't imagine it's easy feeling like you're losing control," he said finally.

His insight shocked her. That he'd given a thought to how she must be feeling also took her by surprise. Was he, too, trying to breach the barrier he'd erected?

She curled her hands into fists and marshaled her thoughts. "It isn't. And it isn't easy every time you try to take it away."

"Honestly, that wasn't my intention." He pulled off at an unexpected exit.

"Where are we going?"

"Somewhere neutral. You've been cooped up for weeks. I'd think you'd welcome fresh air and the great outdoors."

She couldn't help but smile. "Don't be nice to me, Kevin. It makes it too hard to stay angry."

"Then don't."

The reservoir by Boston College loomed in front of them. Kevin pulled into an empty parking spot. After putting the car into park, he leaned an arm over the wheel and turned to face her. Can we call a truce? Let's take a walk, get some fresh air and talk."

She smiled. "I think I can manage that."

"Good. And one more thing. Whatever comes up, remember I have your best interests at heart. Yours and the baby's."

Nikki nodded. He always had the baby's best interest at heart. Hers, too. And up until now, it hadn't been enough. But if she wanted more from him than he was giving now, she'd have to begin accepting his overtures. Start somewhere.

She met him outside the car and together they walked along a graveled path. Green grass spread out before her, water rippled to her left, and blue sky dazzled her overhead. On a day like this, she could almost forget her problems.

Almost, but not quite.

Especially when Kevin placed his hand in hers and squeezed tightly. His strength had a calming effect and the butterflies in her stomach eased. He obviously wanted to talk. She told herself there was nothing he could say that she couldn't handle and hoped she was right.

He paused by a large rock and she curled up on top of it. The smooth surface felt warm and solid through her denim jeans.

"Let's start with basics, okay? Are you comfortable with Dr. Molloy?" Kevin asked.

"Yes. Very. But not with you paying for her private fees."

"I can understand that. And I'm not looking to control your life, but there's not just you to consider." He leaned against the rock beside her. "You may have to come to terms with the fact that I'm half responsible for this situation and since you didn't plan it, you're going to have to accept my help."

She bit down on her lower lip. As much as it pained her to take steps backward and accept help after she'd struggled to be independent, what choice did she have? She couldn't afford everything this baby would need, at least not yet.

"Go on," she said, wanting to hear him out.

"I did some research into my insurance policy through work."

"And?"

"Much as I'd love to cover you, there's no way your pregnancy wouldn't be considered preexisting.

She'd known that already. "Besides, even if they would cover the pregnancy, we'd have to be married in order for coverage to kick in." She glanced down and kicked at a rock on the grass. Better than facing Kevin when mentioning marriage and commitment.

"I know."

"You do?"

He met and held her gaze. "Yes."

Her breath caught as his words sunk in. "You considered marrying me?"

"I still am." If she weren't already sitting down, she might have passed out.

She cautioned herself to be calm. And not to read too much into mere words. "Why? Because it's the right thing to do?"

"Hell, yeah it's the right thing to do. And if Tony...

"If Tony were alive he'd follow you to the church with a shotgun," she finished for him. "But he's not. And not everyone who gets pregnant gets married."

"No, but the smart ones do. Or at least they consider it."

Remain rational, remain calm, Nikki cautioned herself. He didn't know it, but he was handing her the solution she sought. A way to solidify things between them and create a future.

He was going out of his way to do right by her and the baby. So what if she'd rather him profess his undying love and tell her he couldn't live without her. Those were girlish daydreams. And she *had* envisioned marrying Kevin and the reason had nothing to do with an unexpected pregnancy and everything to do with love. If she waited for that to happen, she'd be old and gray first. But if she let him make the decision to commit—and then went backward to build up on that, they might have a chance.

She swallowed hard. "Okay, tell me why marriage would be a benefit?" she said.

He shot her a startled glance. Obviously he expected more of an argument. She was shocking herself, too.

"I can cover the baby without marriage, but he'd still have the stigma of illegitimacy. And I want my... our baby to have my name. To know who his father is, and know he can count on me."

"He?" Nikki couldn't help but chime in.

Kevin grinned. "As soon as *he* or *she* is born."

Logically, she wanted the same things for their

child. But marrying Kevin... tying herself to him for better for worse... forever... she wasn't ready.

"I need time to think," she murmured. She wanted—needed—personal time to digest the concept and the changes that would inevitably follow should she say yes.

"I realize that. But Nikki..." Reaching out, he grasped her chin in his hand and turned her head to face him. "Just know I trust you to make the right decision. For all of us."

He trusted her judgment. A huge concession for a man who feared ceding control. Who feared the consequences if he backed off. "Thank you."

He nodded.

As sure as the breeze blew around her, Nikki knew Kevin's proposal was motivated by devotion to his child. Although she found comfort in his sense of responsibility, she also found pain. Because she'd inadvertently trapped him, and in doing so, she'd found herself someone's responsibility, yet again.

NINE

K evin kicked back in his office and stared at his messages. A couple of offers for freelance security jobs thanks to Patrick O'Neill, a friend on the force, who routinely recommended him for work. Other than Tony, Pat was the only other guy Kevin trusted in a pinch. He was the only person, other than his father, Kevin had let know the moment he hit town again a few months ago.

He glanced at the messages, knowing he'd call these people back. A job was a job. Something to pay the bills. Who was he kidding? Nothing could compete with his previous occupation. He'd loved being a cop. It was in his blood. But Tony's death had changed everything. In the instant he'd seen his partner lying on the ground, Kevin realized he had no business playing backup to anyone. So no matter how much he missed active police work, he was better off consulting on security systems and guarding a warehouse as opposed to a living, breathing human being.

Whether he was fulfilled or not didn't matter.

He had two people relying on him now. Nikki and, soon, his child. That was enough responsibility.

His father had failed at the same responsibility— but Kevin didn't plan to repeat his father's mistakes.

The old man had been quiet since the incident with the neighbor's dog. Too quiet, considering Kevin had threatened to stop paying his rent unless Max became steadily employed again. He often wondered if a quiet Max meant more trouble than a rowdy one.

After booking appointments, he stored the phone numbers and tossed the messages in the trash. With no other business matters to occupy his mind, his thoughts turned to Nikki.

And to his proposal. A marriage of necessity. One made in the best interests of both Nikki and his child. But it would still be a legal union with a woman who drew him in like no other. Who tempted his resolve and tested him at every turn. Who deserved so much better than what life had thrown her way. Including him.

* * *

Now that she was allowed back on her feet, Nikki made productive use of her time. She'd spent the morning at the local library, looking into alcoholism and ways to deal with the family of alcoholics—since she was about to become part of one. And she'd put in a call to her career guidance counselor at school to discuss options, and ways for her to finish her student teaching. He promised to do some research and get back to her.

Hours later, feeling good, she walked around Kevin's place, determined to make it a real home. Mrs. Reid kept the house clean, but domestic touches were missing. It didn't take money to convey warmth and personality, to make an empty, rambling house a place Kevin would want to return to each night.

After digging through her personal things, she added special touches she was sure Kevin had never thought of. Ones she hoped he would notice and appreciate. Flowers were next on the agenda. She'd noticed some beautiful azaleas out back. The outside of the house was a place she'd love to cultivate, but not until the pregnancy was over and strenuous activity was allowed. In the meantime, she decided to work from the inside out.

A sense of boredom? A need for fulfillment? A nesting urge born of the hormonal rush during pregnancy? Nikki shook her head and laughed. Why not call it what it was. Anything to keep busy and to avoid thinking about Kevin's proposal.

Though she didn't like putting him off, she figured she was allowed thinking time before verbally committing to a life-altering decision. Besides, he couldn't be in that big a rush to make a commitment he'd avoided making before.

With scissors in hand, she headed outside. A spring breeze rippled through the air and after being cooped up for so long, the fresh outdoors felt good. Half an hour later, she'd cut her flowers and weeded a small area in the back, all without overexerting herself. Well, not too much. But the sense of exhilaration she got from good old-fashioned yard work and the hour in the sun had done wonders for her mood. The blood was pumping through her veins in a healthy way she hadn't experienced in a very long time.

She headed back around front. After placing the flowers in strategic rooms around the house, she'd do the smart thing and kick her feet up for awhile. At the same time she hit the bluestone path, an unfamiliar truck pulled into the driveway.

She didn't recognize the make or model, and Kevin hadn't mentioned anyone coming to do work in the house. She glanced down at her dirty shirt, grass-stained knees and mud-caked hands and cringed. If she was lucky, this was a repairman Kevin had forgotten to mention, not a friend or neighbor upon whom she'd want to make a good first impression. Nothing she could do about it, regardless, so she took a deep breath and walked to the driveway.

From the minute she saw her visitor up close, she knew that the man was Kevin's father. The differences were as striking as the similarities. Same dark hair, same haunting black eyes, and same handsome features. But the older man's looks had dimmed over the years, due less to age, Nikki suspected, than hard, unhappy living. The lines in his face, and circles and puffy bags under his eyes were glaring, as was the paunch in his stomach. Yet she found herself wanting this man to like her *because* he was Kevin's father.

"Hi." She wiped her hands on her leggings— leggings she'd begun wearing because the elastic felt better than the tight jeans. Apparently nature had taken over sooner than she'd thought. "Nikki Welles." She held her hand out in greeting.

"Hey there." He accepted her hand. He also looked her over from head to toe. "Max Manning. Do I have the wrong house? My boy didn't mention any female roommates or girlfriends or anything."

She shook her head. "This is Kevin's house." She didn't know whether to be insulted he hadn't told his father about their situation or relieved she'd been granted a reprieve. "We're…" She decided to leave the explanations alone for now. "Kevin should be home from work soon. Did he know you were coming by?"

He shook his head. "I wanted to surprise him. He hasn't invited his old man over and I wanted to see what he's done with my sister's house."

Obviously the relationship wasn't a close one, which Nikki had already surmised from the lack of discussion or contact between the two men since she'd moved in. "Would you like to come in and wait for him?"

She didn't want to be rude, but she was curious about this man whom Kevin didn't talk about.

"Don't mind if I do."

She nodded and led the way inside, wondering what Kevin's reaction would be to finding his father here. She hoped she wasn't inviting trouble, yet she could hardly leave the man waiting on the street.

"Why don't you have a seat. Can I get you something to…" Nikki swallowed the rest recalling Kevin's description of his father, though he seemed perfectly sober now. Besides, she couldn't remember seeing alcohol of any kind in the kitchen. "Can I get you anything?" she asked.

"Just water would be fine."

"Sure thing. Make yourself comfortable and I'll be right back." Nikki headed into the kitchen, poured water from a pitcher she kept in the refrigerator, and filled a bowl with sour cream and onion chips from the pantry.

The phone rang and she grabbed it, pleased to find Janine on the other end. She spared a worried glance at the den, then decided his father would understand if she took a few minutes to take a long distance phone call.

But Janine was full of information and a few minutes turned into ten. Nikki returned to the den to find it empty. She placed the glass and bowl of chips down on the table and shrugged. He said he'd come to take a look around, so he couldn't have gone far. Minutes later, she heard footsteps on the stairs leading to the basement. The door opened wide and Max Manning stepped through. "Just wanted to check out the basement. See if my sister hung onto anything of interest."

Nikki narrowed her gaze. As far as she knew, the only things in the basement were mousetraps and a… wine cellar. Damn. She studied him carefully but he looked no worse for his short visit downstairs. Perhaps she was being paranoid. Maybe there was no liquor in the basement and even if there was, how much trouble could he get into in ten minutes?

"I brought you the water and some chips."

"Thanks." He sat down on the couch and Nikki settled herself into her recliner. "So tell me what your relationship is to my boy."

She raised an eyebrow. "You don't beat around the

bush, do you?" she asked.

"Can't see any point in that."

"Okay… we're… good friends." She hoped her nose didn't start to grow. Lately, she and Kevin hadn't shared much in the way of heart-to-heart talks, so she couldn't really classify them as *friends* anymore. Though that was another thing she hoped to change.

The older man's snort told her she'd been found out. "I've been around the block long enough. Try again and let's see if I believe you." He grinned, letting her know he meant no harm, but intended to get an answer.

The sound of a key in the lock saved her from having to answer. Kevin, she thought, and held her breath, not knowing what kind of reaction to expect.

Max's eyes darted toward the door. When Nikki heard the slam, she knew he'd entered the house.

"So you didn't answer. What's your relationship to my son? Girlfriend? Roommate? Lover?"

A heated blush rose to her cheeks.

"Lay off her, Max." Kevin turned the corner into the family room. His gaze darted from Max to Nikki, to the table with refreshments, and back to Max again. "And tell me what the hell you're doing here."

She sucked in a deep breath and steeled herself for what lay ahead. Max had obviously timed his question to coincide with Kevin's entry and she understood

Kevin's gut reaction to the crass question. What she didn't understand was why Max had chosen to act out, when he'd been at least diplomatic up until now.

She'd been right to be concerned about Kevin's reaction to finding his father here. Max Manning wasn't going to make this a comfortable visit. Neither, she assumed, was Kevin.

* * *

Kevin should have known the silence meant trouble. He should have anticipated Max's behavior. When ignored *and* threatened in his pocketbook, Max lashed out. If he couldn't use his fists, he'd find other means. So here he was, searching for trouble.

One glance at Nikki's concerned expression and Kevin knew Max had accomplished his goal. He had no idea how much damage had been done in the time Nikki had been alone with the old man. Judging from his clear gaze, Max was sober. That was something, at least.

If he'd bothered to think about it, he'd have realized he couldn't keep Max and Nikki apart forever, but he'd have liked to try. "I didn't hear an answer," Kevin said to his father.

Max rose from his seat. "Is it a crime to visit my son? For damn sure you wouldn't have invited me."

And that ought to tell you something, Kevin thought.

But Max only saw things one way. His own. "It would have helped if you'd called first."

"Like it would have mattered. You've been living here how long and I've never stepped foot inside."

Nikki jumped to her feet. "Kevin, can I get you a club soda?" she asked.

"No boy of mine drinks that sissy stuff. Get him a beer."

Kevin shot his father a warning look. "There's no alcohol in the house."

"Why not? I don't come by, so you can't be keeping the stuff from me."

Nikki met his gaze, her violet eyes wide with curiosity. No doubt she'd been wondering what caused his about-face. During all the football games and holidays he'd spent with her family, he'd always chosen beer.

He shrugged. "I have my reasons," he muttered. Why insult Max by admitting the truth? It wouldn't do either of them any good.

"Afraid you'll end up like your old man?" his father asked.

Kevin rolled his head from side to side in a futile effort to work out the tension brought on by this homecoming. "I'd love a club soda," he said, hating to have Nikki wait on him, but wanting any excuse to get her out of his father's presence.

She smiled. "No problem. Max? Can I get you

more water?"

"No thanks. It's only making me thirsty for a real drink."

She glanced Kevin's way, obviously unsure how to react. He gave her a small nod and she left for the kitchen. And Kevin turned to Max.

To his shock, he realized he was embarrassed to have Nikki meet his father. He wasn't sure what that said about him as a person, but he knew what it said about Max.

"Are you going to tell me what your relationship is with the pretty lady?" Max asked, his gaze following Nikki as she headed into the kitchen.

"If you'd asked that way the first time, maybe I'd have answered you," Kevin said.

His father shrugged, but his cheeks flushed deep red. "That was uncalled for. I just wanted to get your attention," he muttered.

"Don't tell me you're sorry, tell Nikki."

The older man nodded. "Maybe I will. So she's your what?"

Persistence ran in the family, Kevin thought. Max would find out soon enough. "The mother of my unborn child," he admitted. Another realization blindsided him. If he and Max had ever shared a normal father/son relationship, Kevin might have confided in him earlier. He might have asked for his advice. Instead, Kevin had always played father figure while Max acted the role of immature child.

For once, Kevin found himself hoping this time would be different. Hoped Max would show signs of caring for Kevin—the way Kevin cared for him.

He stared hard at his father, hoping to see some redeeming signs. Signs that would help Kevin face his upcoming role with some degree of certainty that he had it in him to be a decent father. Because he suspected there was some decency left in his own old man.

"I hope you're planning to marry her," Max said. Then he grew silent.

Kevin was surprised as well as grateful. "I am." If she even wanted him.

Max nodded.

"Now what's this visit really about?" Kevin asked him.

"I wanted to see where you're living now. I wanted to visit my son." Max met his gaze. "And to thank you for cleaning up my mess the other night."

A part of Kevin wanted to believe his father, while the weary part of him that had seen this routine before fought against it. Before he could answer, Nikki rejoined them, a glass of club soda in hand.

"I defrosted chicken for dinner and there's enough rice," she said, her wary gaze darting between Kevin and his father.

She'd surprised him again. Mrs. Reid had done all the cooking since she'd been hired. He didn't expect or want Nikki to make his meals. And she'd picked a hell of a day to start—not that she could have anticipated Max.

Kevin stifled a groan. What he didn't need was Nikki playing mediator. He and his father had had perhaps their first civilized conversation ever. He didn't want to push things too far or expect too much.

"I'd like to stay… if I'm welcome," Max said, as if daring Kevin to object now.

"Kevin?" Nikki asked, deferring to him. Once again, he found himself at a loss. Unsure of how to handle this woman who seemed to have taken over his home—and his life.

One day at a time, he decided. He wasn't capable of much more.

Hoping he didn't regret his decision, Kevin turned to Max. "I'd like you to stay, too."

*   *   *

She'd made a huge mistake. Nikki didn't know why she'd gotten involved, why she'd invited Max to stay for dinner. She'd caught glimpses of his belligerent, nastier side, but then she'd overheard him apologize and be sort of sweet to his son. And she'd turned into a marshmallow. The first dinner ever she'd prepared for Kevin—and she invited company.

Was there something subconscious involved there, she wondered wryly. So here she was, with Kevin on one side—and a now drunken Max on the other.

She toyed with the rice on her plate. Kevin had insisted on helping her in the kitchen while Max watched television in the family room. Time had gotten away from them and at least forty minutes had passed. She'd been so on edge about the entire evening, she'd forgotten Max's earlier trip downstairs. Apparently, Max hadn't. And, apparently, there was more in the basement than just wine. Because Kevin's father was rip-roaring drunk.

"Do you want to just drive him home?" Nikki asked, softly.

Kevin shook his head. "Let him eat and maybe he'll sober up," he said, disgust evident in his tone.

She sighed. She felt so responsible for the way the evening had turned out. If only she hadn't invited him for dinner. If only... She shook her head. If only wouldn't change a thing. She'd do her apologizing later, but she had to help Kevin through this meal first.

She pushed her plate aside. Her appetite had fled the minute she'd come into the family room to find Max and a nearly empty bottle of whiskey. "The coffee should be ready. Let me go check."

Max stuffed a forkful of rice into his mouth. "Don't need any."

"But you'll drink it if you know what's good for you."

Nikki rose from her seat. She knew she was better off getting the coffee than remaining in here with Max.

"She doesn't look like she's having a baby."

Nikki froze. Although she knew Kevin had told his father about... their situation, she wasn't sure what an intoxicated Max would say about it.

"Go on and get the coffee, Nikki," Kevin said.

She didn't take offense at the order but her legs wouldn't move. She wanted to hear what came next, certain that Max wouldn't disappoint her.

He laughed loud and hard, but his tone had turned malicious. So were his words. "But if she's set up house here, she must be. Told you you're like your old man. Trapped before your time."

Nikki cringed, realizing for the first time what kind of household Kevin had grown up in. Understanding now why he was so withdrawn, and comprehending why he felt the need to protect and turned on himself when he failed.

That Max's drunken words echoed her own fears wasn't lost on her either. Kevin stood. "Instead of the coffee, just bring me the car keys," he said, never taking his gaze off his father.

Nikki jumped at the chance to get the older man out of the house. When she returned, she handed Kevin the keys and he steered his father toward the front door. "Wasn't done with my meal," he muttered.

"You were done a long time ago," Kevin retorted.

When they reached the door, Max glanced over his shoulder. "He might think he's high and mighty and better than me, but the apple don't fall far from the tree. You both remember that."

Kevin gave him an abrupt shove out and the door slammed closed behind them. The sound of the car engine reached her ears. Wrapping her arms around herself, Nikki shivered. No matter how far away Max got, his parting words continued to echo in the empty house and in Nikki's ears.

Not because Nikki believed him, but because she was all too afraid that Kevin did.

*   *   *

Kevin deposited Max face down in his bed, fully dressed, then headed on home. Facing Nikki tonight would be harder than looking in the mirror each morning, and that was saying a lot. But putting it off wouldn't change the fact that his father was a drunk and had made a despicable scene. He'd also uttered truths Kevin would have preferred remained unspoken. But what the hell. It was nothing Nikki didn't already know.

And, if by chance, she'd started believing in fairy tales, tonight had dispelled the myth. So perhaps he owed Max for that. He stepped into the darkened house, expecting to find himself alone, Nikki closed in her room. He didn't figure she wanted to look at him any more than he'd be able to meet her violet eyes. Eyes he was sure would be filled with pity or disgust. He couldn't tolerate either.

Though the house was quiet and the overhead lights were off, the soft glow of a lamp beckoned to him from the family room. Just like Nikki to be thoughtful and leave a light burning for him, he thought.

With a weary groan, Kevin stepped inside the room.

"Are you okay?" Nikki asked.

Her soft voice took him by surprise.

Kevin was used to Max. She wasn't. He glanced her way. "Are you?"

She bit down on her lower lip. "I feel responsible. He went into the basement earlier and I forgot to mention it... what with dinner and the tension, not that there's an excuse..."

"Stop right there." He held a hand up to forestall any more explanations.

"I don't blame you for being angry."

He raised an eyebrow. "If I'm angry at anyone, it's at myself for subjecting you to him."

"Don't you think he's responsible for his own behavior, not you?"

Kevin couldn't help but grin. "Using that logic, you ought to lighten up on yourself, too."

She tipped her head to one side. "So you're not upset with me."

"No, Nikki. I'm not upset with you." How could he be? She was the one person who made him want to be better than he was—and the one person he kept letting down.

"But you're still upset."

"You always were perceptive."

"I'm also here. For you."

Though he'd be damned later, Kevin couldn't resist the temptation—or the solace she offered. She held out her arms and he walked into her embrace.

* * *

No hesitation, no uncertainty. One minute Nikki was standing alone, the next he was there. She had no illusions. Kevin needed someone. If he hadn't been emotionally drained, he'd never have turned to her now.

But somehow, it didn't matter. Solid and sexy, his hard body aligned with hers, leaving no doubt where this could lead.

If she so desired.

She cupped his cheeks in her hands. *If she desired.* As if wanting him was ever in question. She'd sought the chance to show him what they could share. It seemed she was getting her wish in a way she'd never expected. Maybe she'd regret this in the morning. Or maybe she'd be looking at a brand-new start.

What better way for them to begin again than with the ultimate act of intimacy? If nothing else, they were good at that. Good at giving of themselves when the other one was in pain. What was so wrong with that? Didn't that show a depth of caring not many people possessed?

He grabbed her wrists. "You know we shouldn't do this."

"Why not? It's not like I could get pregnant," she said with a grin.

Her attempt at lightening the situation worked, and Kevin laughed. But only for a moment. "I'm no good for you, Princess."

"Why don't you let me be the judge of what's good for me?" she asked. Her body ached in delicious ways and all because she was in his arms, inhaling his scent and imagining them entwined more deeply. She drew a breath for courage and pressed closer to him.

He let out a slow groan. "Nikki…"

"No more words, okay?" She touched her mouth to his. His lips were warm, but remained closed.

After seeing his father in action, Nikki understood how Kevin's mind worked. He'd never had anyone give to him or take care of him. Rather, he'd always been the strong one. Which was why he possessed that all-consuming need to control. About why he tended to treat people like they needed his protection.

"I don't need your protection," she murmured. She threaded her fingers through his hair, feeling the soft strands between her fingertips. "But I do need you."

* * *

A man couldn't resist a plea like that—even if the reverse were true. Nikki didn't need Kevin as much as Kevin needed her. She was warm and giving, and she wanted him. She wasn't holding his father's behavior against him, nor did she seem disgusted by tonight's scene.

She seemed only concerned...for him.

And he needed that right now. Needed her. He cupped her face in his hands, much as she'd done to him. And he kissed her the way she demanded to be kissed. Her mouth opened in return and he lost himself in her.

Their clothes landed haphazardly around the

room. Wanting more for Nikki than a fast tumble, he swept her off her feet.

"You do realize you're lifting two of us," she said, laughing.

"Do you hear me complaining?"

"I hope we're going to bed," she murmured. Her tone was sexy, her eyes glazed with desire.

"Can't argue with that." And he couldn't. Not with them both undressed. The warmth of her skin heated his already overloaded senses. They made it to the bedroom and he lowered her to the bed before following her. At least the sheets were cool, a contrast to the fever burning inside him.

Kevin felt the give and take between them, sensed the need when he cupped her breast in his hand. The soft mound was fuller now than last time and the reason why was staggering.

With every movement and every touch, he was in tune to Nikki. But he couldn't escape the feeling in his gut that they weren't meant to be. That this time was inevitable, but it couldn't... *shouldn't* happen again. And from the frenzied way she writhed against him, he had a hunch she knew it, too.

TEN

T he aftershocks of her climax had barely subsided when Kevin rolled off her. "Don't want to crush you," he muttered.

Nikki didn't believe him. More like he didn't want to be inside her once his brain kicked back into gear and he'd have to face what he was feeling. She inhaled and refused to give in to despair. The seductive masculine scent that was so much a part of him wrapped itself around her, giving her strength.

She wouldn't give up a possible future. Not without a fight. She wasn't sure when she'd made the decision. She did know she'd been struggling with it, fighting an internal battle between what was best for her baby and what was safest for her heart. There was no contest as to which was more important.

The scene with his father should have convinced her to back off and have nothing to do with him. After all, she'd seen why he couldn't sustain relationships easily and knew what a struggle it would be to force him to try. He'd had no family to speak of growing up and she didn't want her child raised with an absent father, or worse, none at all.

If she were to give her baby the sense of family she'd had, if she was going to give all of them that feeling of family, she'd have to start at the beginning. She reached for his hand and brought it to rest on the slight swell of her stomach, which felt like it had blossomed overnight. "You can feel the baby kick as early as fourteen weeks," she said.

She met his gaze. No doubt he'd been expecting her to question his emotions or the reasons he'd backed off. But an overt grasp for his heart wouldn't work. Instead, she planned to ambush him slowly until his heart and hers were so closely intertwined he couldn't tell whose was beating stronger, or faster. Until he didn't want to.

"It's too soon then." His fingers curled more tightly against her stomach. More possessively, she thought.

"It's too soon," she agreed. "But a few more weeks and it won't be." She looked into his dark eyes. "Will you want to feel it? Or will you want to run?"

He lay a hand over his forehead and covered his eyes. "You don't ask for much, do you?"

Now that their lovemaking was over and the world had intruded, a chill rushed over her skin. "I'm not asking for anything at all." She tugged at the bedsheet until it covered her exposed skin. The cotton was cool and did nothing to warm her, so she curled into Kevin's body heat. The chill eased completely. She wasn't surprised.

"I helped create this life. You know I want to be part of everything." He wrapped his arm around her waist. Because she'd pushed first or not, she'd never know.

"I didn't know or I wouldn't have asked. But that aside, there was more of a point to the question."

"What is it?"

"If you want to share in the physical changes in my body, we're going to have to come to some kind of understanding," Nikki said.

Kevin bolted upright beside her. "What kind of understanding?" he asked warily.

"I'll marry you, Kevin. I'll give my baby his father's name and the best possible medical care. I'll give you a home and try to be the best wife I can be. I only ask one thing in return." She had a nerve asking anything at all, she knew. He was doing all the giving just to make her life—and their baby's life—easier.

"Why do I think giving blood would be easier than whatever's on your mind?" he muttered. "You have to know I'll do whatever it takes to keep both of you safe."

She sighed. So it all came down to that again. To responsibility. What she wanted from him entailed so much more. "Safety isn't the issue, Kevin."

She curled her legs beneath her. Being naked around him didn't embarrass her, which said so much about her trust and faith in him. Why couldn't he see that?

They sat in silence. He obviously waited for her to continue. She couldn't ask him to love her. Either he did or he didn't.

She hung her head for a minute, gathering her thoughts. "A baby should be born into an atmosphere of peace and harmony. Into a family," she explained at last.

*　　*　　*

She raised her head and Kevin met her gaze. "Like I said… you don't ask much, do you?" She didn't just want what he could give her or the baby. She wanted his heart and soul. His heart was rusty from disuse and aged beyond his years, while his soul was something he'd discarded when Tony died.

She might as well have asked him to cut himself in two. But he had to admit he'd set himself up for this. Every move he'd made had been an uncalculated step in this direction. Sleeping with Nikki, getting her pregnant, asking her to move in, and insisting they marry.

And now she wanted it all—the white picket fence and the family out of a Norman Rockwell painting. How could he expect a woman like Nikki, a wholesome woman from a close-knit family, to want anything less? He actually envied her wide-eyed optimism.

If she thought he was capable of making the attempt, how could he deny her? "You really think someone like me can give you what you want?" he asked.

She nodded. "All I want," she said softly, "is you."

That's what he was afraid of. "When?" he asked.

She inhaled and a visible shudder rippled through her. So she wasn't any more sure of this arrangement than he. "As soon as possible."

He wondered if she was still trying to convince herself marrying him was the right thing to do. He couldn't blame her. As soon as possible would prevent either of them from changing their minds—or running from their feelings.

As soon as possible was the right thing for everyone. He nodded. "Next weekend work for you?" he asked.

Wide-eyed, she gave a small nod of assent. He

looked into those violet eyes. Eyes that shimmered with emotion and brimmed with tears. No way were they tears of joy. She was stuck with him.

But they'd made their bed almost three months ago. It was time to sleep in it. Damning himself for a fool, he pulled her into his arms.

*   *   *

Nikki had to hand it to Kevin—he hadn't been avoiding the house, nor had he been avoiding her. If his presence was all she wanted, then she'd have to say he'd been trying. Just as she'd asked.

Just as he'd promised.

But his emotions had remained firmly in check and, despite her best efforts, she hadn't been able to tap into them. With their wedding two days away, Nikki felt as though the minutes of her life were ticking down. She was marrying the man she'd dreamed of marrying, but for all the wrong reasons.

All the wrong *personal* reasons, she amended. She placed her hand over her stomach and wondered when the nervous jitters would turn into the real flutters described in the books. She couldn't wait to feel her baby kick. Evidence of life symbolized hope. She'd do anything for the happiness and security of this child, even if it meant risking her heart.

When she heard Kevin's key turn in the lock, she

braced herself for the inevitable awkwardness between them. Kevin surrounded himself with mile-high barriers. It would have felt like an icy reserve, if she hadn't known better. Because that chill wasn't ever-present. At night beneath the covers, the chill evaporated, replaced by a sizzling heat.

They shared more than just the same double bed in her room. Way beyond sex, she and Kevin connected in a meaningful way. He engaged her heart and soul, and she was able to let herself go. Because she was giving herself to Kevin, and he to her. When he was inside her, he didn't hold himself back on any level. He gave of himself endlessly. She wanted to grab onto that closeness and bring it into the light of day.

So far, she hadn't been successful. She supposed she should be grateful there was any time at all when she could breach his reserve, get past his fear and distrust. Not of Nikki, but of himself. The irony wasn't lost on her. If he hadn't trusted her, she could work to prove herself to him, but how could she get him to believe in himself? In his own worthiness, when the man who'd raised him was a constant reminder of his so-called failures.

"Nikki?" His voice called out from the hall.

"In my room." Although he'd wanted her to move into the master bedroom where she'd be more comfortable—or so he'd *said*, she'd insisted on waiting until they were married. In her mind, it was another way to make the distinction between "individual" and "couple" mean something to Kevin.

Since she'd been able to reach him in bed, his bedroom, the place where they would begin their married life, that was the place she would start. A resourceful woman could work with that, and in the last couple of months, Nikki had learned to be more resourceful than she'd ever dreamed she could be.

* * *

"Hi there." Kevin walked into her dimly lit room. Nikki sat with an open magazine on her lap, the glow of a small bedside lamp illuminating her delicate features.

Ever since they'd made their decision, she appeared more serene and calm than he could admit to being. Not because he wanted to back out, but because he was waiting for her to do it first.

She glanced at the small digital clock on the nightstand. "Is everything okay? You're usually home much earlier." Her hand curled around the comforter in a tight fist. "I didn't mean I was keeping tabs on you or anything. I just meant that…"

He let out a long breath of air. "I didn't think you were checking up on me."

"Everything okay at work?"

He nodded. "I stopped by to see Max." Not because he wanted to but because he couldn't live with himself if he didn't make sure his old man was okay.

"How's he doing?"

"He wasn't there." Kevin had a hunch where he could have found his father, but he wasn't in the mood to hit the seedy bars downtown.

She patted the empty side of the bed. "Sit down and relax," she murmured.

Every day, he promised himself he wouldn't climb into bed with Nikki and selfishly take what she so unselfishly offered. But he couldn't stop himself—and she didn't seem to mind. If anything, the stiltedness between them dissolved each time he joined her beneath the covers.

She'd asked him to make an effort at doing the family thing. But he wasn't comfortable sharing his feelings over the dinner table, as he'd never grown up with a family who ate together or discussed their daily events. No one really cared about anything except tiptoeing around his old man's moods and temper.

Yet, as soon as he joined Nikki in bed, the discomfort dissolved and barriers dropped. He hoped she was satisfied with that because he couldn't offer any more. He just didn't know how.

At her prompting, he sat down on top of the comforter. She turned toward him and drew her legs up to rest her chin on her knees. He met her gaze and she extended her hand. Meet me halfway, she seemed to be asking.

And there was nothing he wanted more.

Before he could take her hand, the jarring ring of the telephone shattered the peaceful, welcome silence. And after he'd taken the call, he knew peace was like hope. Both damn illusions.

*   *   *

Kevin could swear he heard his heart pounding during the entire half-hour trip into Boston. By the time he parked, he'd worked up a good sweat. He'd seen Max in many situations, but flat on his back in a hospital bed would be a new one.

When they got inside, the emergency room of the hospital was bustling with people. Kevin stopped at the sign-in desk. "I'm here to see Max Manning."

The harassed-looking woman behind the desk glanced down at a clipboard filled with names and other information. "Are you immediate family?" she asked.

"Yes."

Nikki slipped her hand inside his and squeezed once. He appreciated the reassurance. He wasn't sure he would have been able to make it through this without her by his side. Seeming to understand, she hadn't said a word. After he'd hung up the phone, she'd just climbed out of bed and dressed so she could accompany him to the hospital—where she'd get to witness yet another reason why she shouldn't want or expect anything from Kevin Manning.

"Through those doors and ask at the desk inside," the woman said, then turned to the next person on line behind them.

They stepped aside. "Maybe I should have had him move into the house," Kevin muttered. But he'd escaped hell once, and he hadn't wanted to live with Max ever again. Selfish, Kevin knew. Because now his father lay passed out in a hospital bed.

"You can't stop a drunk from drinking," Nikki said, reminding him of his own words.

He shrugged. She was right, but damned if he could shake the nagging notion that he could have prevented this. Just like he could have prevented Tony's death. *If he'd just been there.* "I'd better get in to see him."

She nodded in agreement "I'll wait here," she said in an obvious effort to give him space.

He ought to take it but couldn't. He gave Nikki's hand a tug and headed through the emergency room doors, uncertain what he'd find. What he found was Max, looking sallow and appearing to be out cold in a small cubicle enclosed by a curtain similar to the one found in bathtub showers.

Kevin shook his head. Change the scenery and the hospital bed, and this could have been Max's living room couch. "Is he okay?" Kevin asked the attending nurse.

"He's stable. The doctor will be by with more information later. He's resting comfortably now."

He nodded. "Thanks."

Kevin walked to the bed and stood over his father. He couldn't say the man had raised him. By sheer luck and a sainted mother, he'd survived. And he had to admit, just by looking at Max, he'd survived well. He hadn't thought so up till now, but at least he hadn't ended up a drunk like his old man, and that was saying something.

Kevin's childhood had been a nightmare. Though he wanted so much more for his child than he'd been given, he didn't know if he was capable of providing it. All he'd managed so far was one letdown after another.

But Nikki had asked him to try. Looking at his father now, Kevin knew he'd have to give more than he'd managed so far. He'd have to be there for them both.

He only hoped it would be enough.

* * *

Nikki woke up alone in her bed. Because Kevin had been adamant, she'd taken a taxi home from the hospital so she could get a decent night's sleep on a comfortable mattress. For the baby's sake, and for Kevin's peace of mind, she'd agreed, but she hadn't left him willingly. She just didn't want to give him something else to worry about when he should be focusing on his father.

After a quick shower and change, she called for a cab and headed back to the hospital. Max had been admitted and Nikki tiptoed into his room so as not to disturb him. But the sight that greeted her was more moving and more disturbing to her than she'd anticipated.

Max lay in much the same position they'd found him in last night, sleeping on his back, an IV sticking out of his arm. But Kevin had fallen asleep in a hardback chair he'd pulled to the side of the bed, no doubt so he could watch over the father he didn't understand.

He was standing guard, Nikki thought, in the protective mode she'd come to know too well. Her heart twisted at the sight. After his admission last night, she understood now why Kevin took his responsibilities so seriously, why he berated himself when something went wrong, and why he insisted on being in control.

To his way of thinking, if he controlled the situation around him, bad things couldn't happen. He really believed his mere presence could prevent fate from intervening. As if anything could, she thought sadly.

But at least she now understood why he felt responsible for Tony's death, why he believed if he'd been there, he could have prevented it. Why he insisted on taking care of her and the baby.

And why she had to allow it. She had to accept him as he was or walk away. A man like Kevin couldn't change.

She touched a hand to his shoulder and he jolted upright. "Sorry," she whispered.

He rubbed his palms over his eyes, reminding her of an exhausted but weary little boy. Yet when he removed his hands and rose to his feet, he was every inch a man. Between the razor stubble, which was more than a day old, and the deep onyx of his eyes, he was the rebel cop she...

Nikki cleared her throat, choking back the word love, unable to cope with the reality of such a strong emotion when she'd just acknowledged that Kevin wouldn't, couldn't change. Not for his child and certainly not for her.

"Is he okay?" She rubbed her hands over her arms. Anything to keep busy and not think about the driving need to comfort him.

He shrugged. "Max had a restless night but what

can you expect when you've ingested that amount of alcohol," he said in disgust.

She nodded. "I brought you a change of clothes."

She lay a plastic bag at the foot of the bed. "And some black coffee. I figured you'd need some."

"Know what I really need?" he asked.

She shook her head.

"You," he said and she walked into his open arms.

Nikki allowed his warmth to envelop her and hoped she gave some of the same strength back to him. They'd need it in the days and months ahead. Because she now knew nothing would play out the way she'd hoped. Mannings are no good for taking care of anyone except themselves. What a misguided legacy Max had passed on to his son.

But this episode with Max had driven home the fact that Kevin would always consider her a responsibility. One he had no choice but to face, but one he feared failing.

Maybe he'd need her for a moment, or a night, but in the end, he'd keep his distance for fear of letting her down, for fear of destroying what he touched. He'd never let himself admit to caring. To loving. To wanting the family she so desperately needed.

Nikki blinked back the tears forming in her eyes. She'd marry Kevin as planned. She'd give her child a name and all the benefits he deserved starting out in life.

But happily ever after wasn't in her future, and she'd put out feelers in case of this eventuality. Now it was time to act accordingly.

ELEVEN

"**I** can't believe I came back in time for a wedding." Janine smoothed the soft petals on Nikki's bouquet. Delicate white lilies spread their fragrant scent throughout the confines of Janine's small car.

True to bridal tradition, Nikki had spent the night before at her sister-in-law's apartment refusing to see Kevin until she arrived at the justice of the peace.

"With his father still in the hospital, we almost canceled." In truth, *she* almost canceled. The thought never crossed Kevin's mind.

She'd desperately wanted to postpone the wedding. She wanted Kevin to go into this day with a clear head. She didn't want him to be able to look back and feel he'd been distracted or that she'd taken advantage of him in any way. But he'd insisted, claiming Max's illness had nothing to do with their future.

Nikki would have laughed at his naïveté if the consequences weren't so dire. Until Kevin accepted the fact that Max had everything to do with not only his outlook on life but his self-perception, they didn't stand a chance of making it through the long haul.

"How is his father, anyway?"

Nikki shrugged. "They should release him in a couple of days. He can't undo the damage the alcohol's done to his liver, but if he stops drinking, he gives himself a chance."

"Will he?"

"The better question is *can* he. It's sad, but I really don't see it happening."

Janine sighed. "You never know. What with you two getting married and a grandchild on the way, he's got good reason to want to stick around."

If Nikki closed her eyes, she could almost imagine the family Janine had just alluded to. Nikki, Kevin, and their baby—and Kevin's father, the only grandparent arriving on Sundays for dinner. Just the thought put a curling warmth inside her.

"Speaking of weddings…" Janine glanced over at Nikki. "I spoke to you last week and you didn't say a thing. Wasn't this an awfully quick decision?" Janine asked.

"Depends on how you look at it." Nikki smoothed the waist of her dress down so her stomach became more visible. "The bride's already pregnant. Some would say it happened too late." She forced a smile, one at odds with the jitters in her stomach.

Janine slowed the car and pulled over to the side of the road. She glanced at Nikki, whose bulky form made turning impossible. "You aren't fooling me, Nicole."

Meeting her sister-in-law's penetrating stare wasn't easy. Nikki wished she could have blamed her inability on the blazing sun. But having reached suburbia, a large tree prevented the sharpest rays from blinding them through the windshield. Besides, fooling Janine wasn't an option. She had always been too perceptive by half, and being pregnant had only intensified her radar when it came to matters of the heart.

"I'm scared to death," Nikki admitted. Once the words had escaped, her body reacted. Her heart began to pound and she broke into a cold sweat.

"Put your head between your knees," Janine suggested.

Nikki shook her head. "I'm not going to faint."

"I nearly did. The day I married your brother, I had my head in a brown paper bag up until right before I walked down the aisle."

"Are you trying to tell me I'm normal?"

Janine laughed. "I'd never say such a thing." She grinned. "What I'm saying is what you're feeling is normal." She shifted position again. "Unless you're truly having second thoughts and not just last-minute jitters."

Nikki bit down on her lower lip.

"Cut it out, you'll eat off your lipstick. Now what's wrong?"

It all came down to the same thing. She wanted the fairy tale wedding. The "to love and to cherish," the happily ever after. With the seconds ticking down, she was forced to look into her heart.

She loved him.

She always had. When she looked at Kevin, her heart raced and blood heated. When he was in pain, she hurt for him, and on the rare occasions when he laughed with her, her heart soared toward the clouds. She loved him, all right. But he didn't reciprocate the emotion.

His sense of duty was strong, so here she was in a cream-colored suit, loose enough in the waist to accommodate her pregnant form. She may not want him coerced into marriage, but what else could she call it? If it weren't for the life growing inside her, she'd run far and fast.

"What is it?" Janine asked.

Nikki met Janine's questioning gaze. "He doesn't love me," she admitted.

"He doesn't know how to show it. There's a difference."

"I wish that were true, but…" She lifted her shoulders, then dropped them again.

"I believe it is, but unless he says the words, what I think doesn't matter." Janine sighed. "Do you want to call it off?"

"For the baby's sake, I can't. And besides, I want to make it work."

What she couldn't explain to Janine was that she was going into this marriage while making contingency plans for herself in case it failed.

Nikki loved Janine like a sister, but her faith in Kevin was strong, her desperation to see Nikki with the man she loved even stronger. Tony's death had reinforced her belief in grabbing happiness while it was still possible. And though Nikki understood, Janine's behavior in the past made trusting her in this case impossible. Besides, in another week, Janine would be packed up and back home.

And Nikki would, once again, be on her own.

"So you're sure about this?" Janine asked.

Nikki closed her eyes, knowing this was her last chance to back out. She took a deep breath before facing Janine. "I'm sure."

Janine glanced at her watch, then shifted gears and placed the car back into drive. "Then we've got a wedding to make."

*   *   *

Kevin paced the floor outside Max's hospital room, debating the merits of whether to go in or turn around and walk away. He wanted to. But that was Max's style, not his.

You walked out on Nicole, a voice in his head taunted. And it sickened him to realize how like his father he'd become. So he pulled open the door and walked inside.

The television blared too loud from the remote speaker buried inside the covers on the bed. Kevin shook his head, wondering if Max even cared. "Hey, Max. How are you feeling?" Kevin yelled above the blaring television.

His father, looking more sallow than ever, pushed himself up against the pillows. He let out a loud whistle, more suited to a construction site than a hospital room. "Where're you going all dressed up like that? Ain't no way I'm the reason you cleaned yourself up."

"I'm getting married," he told his father. And that was the reason for this visit.

Although Kevin had given up on having a real father years ago, he couldn't face this day without at least letting the old man know he was tying the knot. That he intended to make a go of this marriage. Hell, he intended to make a go of his life—despite his parentage.

If he were honest with himself, Kevin knew he wanted his father's blessing—something he'd never get. But here he was anyway, a sucker for punishment.

"Well at least you're doing the right thing," Max muttered.

"Like you did?"

"I never said…"

"You didn't have to." Kevin walked over to the worn plastic chair he'd spent one night in and sat down. Sunlight streamed through the blinds and heated his back. "You reminded Mom that she'd trapped you and destroyed your life every day she lived under your roof."

He shrugged. "Don't think you won't be doing the same thing. Coming home every day to a reminder of how you got tied down."

It shouldn't hurt to hear his father's feelings on parenthood. He'd been exposed to it often enough as a child. Yet on the verge of a major life change himself, Kevin wanted some support. He knew an *I'm proud of you, son* would have been too much to ask for, but he'd have at least liked a pat on the back.

Kevin rose from his seat. "Nikki's not tying me down. Besides it takes two to tango," he reminded his father. Not that Max understood the concept of responsibility.

"Talk to me in a couple a years and you'll feel differently. In the meantime, when are you gonna get me sprung?"

"When the doctor says it's time." Kevin glanced at his watch. "I have a wedding to get to."

"It won't be a party without your old man."

Which was exactly why Kevin had insisted on not postponing the wedding until Max was out of the hospital. He wanted to start his new life with dignity and hope. He wanted to believe he could be the exception to the rule. That *this* Manning could take care of more than just himself, but his wife and child, as well.

He glanced over his shoulder. But if the man lying in the hospital bed was the foundation on which his future—and Nikki's future—had been laid, they were in serious trouble.

*　　*　　*

Kevin paced the floor outside the justice of the peace, wondering if Nikki had finally come to her senses and changed her mind. He wouldn't blame her if she had.

He'd slept alone in his big rambling house last night, for the first time since she had moved in. The loneliness had been overwhelming. Everywhere he turned, he'd seen signs of Nikki. On the kitchen table, a vase filled with freshly cut flowers. On the windows, curtains she'd made herself from a variety of sheets and fabrics. Personal touches that had turned his empty house into a home. He hadn't noticed before and wondered if it was too late now that he had.

Visiting Max had been his way of bridging the past and the present. Now he waited for Nikki and hoped she'd give their future a shot.

By the time Janine's cream-colored car pulled up in front of the small house owned by the man who would marry them, Kevin's sense of relief was palpable. His palms were even damp and he felt like a damn kid asking a girl on a first date. He refused to question why his emotions rode him so strongly. Yes, he wanted the best for his baby and marriage would help provide it, and yes, he needed to know he'd have the opportunity to *be there* for both Nikki and his child. But at some point, marrying Nikki had become important to him for more personal reasons. Reasons he didn't want to deal with at the moment.

She was here and that was all that mattered.

She stepped out of the car and Kevin's breath caught in his throat. By mutual agreement they hadn't planned an elaborate ceremony and he hadn't given much thought to details. Obviously, she had.

Her cream-colored suit contrasted with her jet-black hair and offset her skin. As corny as it sounded, she glowed. He started toward her and realized her cheeks were a bright shade of pink. He wondered if it was the pregnancy or the wedding that had her so flushed.

He stopped in front of her and met her gaze. Those violet eyes were wide and if he wasn't mistaken, she was as anxious as he. Over her shoulder, he saw Janine standing by the car. Obviously, she wanted to give them time alone, but Kevin could have used her distraction right about now.

"You look beautiful," he said.

She reached out and brushed a hand over his one and only suit. Weddings, funerals, command performances—this suit had seen it all. "You look pretty good yourself," she said softly. "Kevin…" She bit down on her lower lip. "Are you sure about this? You could walk away and I wouldn't think any less of you."

"But maybe I would." He grasped her chin in his hand. "Are *you* sure?"

She let out an uncertain laugh. "I wouldn't want these flowers to go to waste."

He glanced down, noticing for the first time the delicate bouquet of white flowers she carried in her hand. He cursed himself for not thinking of that kind of thing, for not knowing the little things that would make her feel special. "Is that the only reason you're going through with this?" he asked.

He knew his reasons for the marriage or at least he

thought he did. Seeing Nikki now, realizing how deep his fear went that she'd back out on him, he wasn't so sure there wasn't more involved here than obligation and responsibility. And that scared him. Because when he let her down—and given his history, there wasn't a question that he would—he'd lose much more than he'd ever imagined. So he needed to know her reasons, and he needed them badly.

She touched his cheek with a shaking hand. "I have many reasons," she murmured. "None you'd be comfortable hearing. But I'm here and I'll do my part to make this work. As long as you do the same."

He nodded. It wasn't the answer he'd hoped for and yet she was right. Anything more and he'd be in deep trouble.

He'd thought of Nikki in a variety of ways over the years. First as Tony's sister, then as the woman he couldn't forget and lately as the mother of his child. He stared into the eyes of his soon-to-be wife. "I'll do my best," he promised her.

He wondered if, like him, she questioned his ability to manage even that.

*   *   *

Nikki stood at the doorway to Kevin's house. Behind her, she felt his solid presence. Her life had changed, yet again, and this time it was for better, for worse, for richer, for poorer, till death us do part. A chill shook her and she trembled.

She felt Kevin's hands on her shoulders, steadying her. To his credit, he'd been just as steady and sure from the moment he'd linked hands with her outside the small house and throughout the brief ceremony. He'd anticipated her emotions and squeezed her hand when she thought of the people who weren't at her wedding—Tony and her parents. He was a good man and the sooner she could get him to realize that, the stronger their chances were at making the marriage work.

"Second thoughts?" he asked.

She shook her head. "None." And she meant it.

"Then you're waiting for me to carry you over the threshold?" he asked, amusement in his voice.

"I'd like to see you..." The rest of her sentence trailed off in a shriek as he swept her off her feet and into his arms.

"Never dare a man, Nicole." Laughter lit his eyes, but so did banked desire.

She knew. She understood. Because she felt it, too. And when they came together this time, they would be husband and wife. Considering the significance, she was amazed at his lighthearted banter. If this was his way of trying, she appreciated the attempt.

Once inside the house and back on her feet, Nikki

took charge. She'd promised herself if she had to walk away, it wouldn't be for lack of trying to make her marriage work. She glanced down at the ring on her left hand. While not a sparkling, glittering diamond, the simple gold band meant more to her than any jewel.

"Disappointed?" he asked.

She shook her head. "It's perfect," she murmured. "Just like the day." Although she'd dreamed of a traditional wedding surrounded by family, those dreams belonged to the child she'd been, not the grown-up she'd become. And the small but intimate ceremony with Janine, Kevin, and the life growing inside her met all her current needs and dreams.

She grabbed for his hand and as he laced their fingers together, a curling ribbon of warmth flowed through her. Just for tonight, Nikki wanted to put all thoughts of the future out of her head. She wanted to focus on the present. Tomorrow she would build from there.

"Come on." He turned toward the hall, giving her hand a light tug.

"Where?" she asked, playing along.

"Come to bed. My bed." His husky voice pulled at her, luring her with its depth and need.

She followed him down the hall, anticipation building with every step. She paused at the entry to the master bedroom. "I thought it was our bed now."

He swept her off her feet again, and deposited her on top of the mattress. As an answer, she supposed it sufficed. And she had to admit, it gave her hope.

He lowered himself over her, bracketing her shoulders with his hands. The intense pull stretched from her breasts downward, where between her legs, a pulsing, throbbing beat picked up a steady rhythm.

His dark eyes bore into hers and she was drawn in all over again. Kevin pulled her up into a sitting position and worked at the buttons on the front of her suit. The lapels of her jacket fell open and slipped off her shoulders.

Nikki shouldn't be embarrassed. Kevin had seen her before, night after night when they'd made love in her bed. But he'd never looked at her as his wife—the woman he'd tied himself to—for as long as they both shall live. Or at least for as long as Nikki could hold onto the hope that lived inside her at this moment.

But she couldn't help the seeds of doubt, the concern that maybe he regretted his decision. "Disappointed?" It was her turn to ask.

He shook his head. "You're perfect. Just like…"

"Don't tease me, Kevin. Not about this."

He grabbed for her hands, which now covered her chest, and pulled them down to her sides. "Look. And see yourself as I see you."

She glanced downward. Her breasts, fuller now than ever before, spilled over the lace cups of her bra. "I guess I can see how they meet with your approval."

His hands cupped her breasts. His darker skin against her whiter flesh, combined with his heated touch, had an erotic effect on her senses. And when his mouth came down hard on hers, concerns about what he thought fled. Because she couldn't mistake the reverent way his hands caressed her body or the deliberate way he made love to her with his mouth.

With every touch, with every shift of his body against hers, he told her she was special. He left no doubt in her mind that he didn't regret his decision and that he wanted her every bit as much as she wanted him. As always, their inhibitions fled beneath the covers, but this time, their union meant so much more. And she prayed that, for once, it would last into the light of tomorrow.

Kevin entered her, creating exquisite friction as every hard ridge of his erection touched the deep recesses of her body. And in the burst of light that followed, Nikki caught a glimpse of her future.

*　　*　　*

Nikki came awake by degrees. A delicious warmth heated her body and a tantalizing masculine scent greeted her with each breath. "Kevin," she murmured.

In response, his hand slid upward to cup her breast. She sighed at the strong touch and buried her face in the crook of his neck while her fingers splayed over his hard length.

He groaned aloud. "Sorry, didn't mean to wake you in the middle of the night," he said, pressing a kiss against her cheek.

The butterfly-light touch whispered against her skin, creating a tingling sensation she didn't want to end. With his other hand, his fingers moved idly across her breast, sending a direct current flaring to life between her legs.

He pulled her closer until she felt the weight of his erection hard against her thighs. She felt his hand on her cheek, his thumb beneath her jaw, stroking and arousing. He really could affect her with the softest touch.

"Look at me, Nikki."

She tilted her head back until she met his steady gaze, dark and filled with need. "I want you."

"I…" His fingers touched her lips, stopping her from expressing her thoughts.

She'd allow him to silence her. For now. Their intimate moments were wonderful but they weren't enough to compensate for the other times. Times when they needed to relate and connect on a deeper level.

She wanted the *possibility* of love… for them both.

There had to be a beginning before there could be a middle or an end. He'd taken a risk by marrying her. She'd have to accept it as a start.

She tipped her head upward and he kissed her lips once before she pulled back, wanting her chance to view him as he'd viewed her last night. She took in the bronzed skin, the dark hair on his chest, and the well-muscled body around which she'd awakened. No wonder she'd been warm. No wonder she was burning up now.

He drew her finger into his mouth and she sucked in a startled gasp, cutting off what she'd been about to say. His teeth and lips grazed her finger, causing an answering pull low in her belly. Relaxing her head against the pillow, she closed her eyes and gave herself up to sensation. To his lips on her face and neck, to his hands on her breasts and stomach. To whisper-soft kisses and gentle caresses that had her sighing with pleasure and moaning with need.

He wrapped his hands around her calves and began kneading the muscles in a firm circular motion, moving upward as he worked. When his strong fingers splayed across her thighs, she stiffened and her eyes opened wide.

"Not relaxed any more, huh?"

She glanced down to where his tanned hands rested against her lighter skin. His thumbs caressed the inside of her thighs, inching upward. "Not quite."

"And after all that hard work," he murmured. "I'll have to do something about that." Pulling himself up, he positioned himself over her, legs touching legs, her breasts beneath his chest and his erection pulsing solidly against her stomach. Her hips jerked upward in response.

She trailed her fingers down his back, savoring the ripple of hard muscle and the contrast of his soft skin. Her hands followed around his waistline to the coarse trail of hair in front.

"God." He exhaled a harsh groan and Nikki felt the strain in his body and the flex of his arms as he struggled to remain in control. And she hadn't even touched him yet.

She'd wanted a chance. Maybe, just maybe she'd gotten one. She pressed a kiss against his throat and followed with a light lick of her tongue. With a harsh groan, he ground his hips against hers in a rough thrust that didn't come near to satisfying the empty ache that had been building inside her. She shifted her legs, raising her hips, desperate to give him what he wanted, to find what she needed. That she'd lost control, as well, didn't matter.

In the back of her mind came the realization that she'd lost something more, something she couldn't possibly get back. She'd lost her heart.

*　　*　　*

Kevin felt the sweat bead on his forehead. The muscles in his arms jerked with the strain of attempting to take things slow. His control hung by a fragile thread. She affected him on so many levels, he couldn't begin to count.

He didn't want to think about what that meant and the only thing to do was bury himself deep inside her willing body. Her moist heat beckoned and blocked out all thoughts other than of the release they both sought.

Lose himself in her again. With Nikki, sex wasn't an impersonal act because she had the ability to reach inside him. As much as he fought the notion, she wasn't just some woman he'd taken to bed. She was his wife, as much by choice as by bargain.

If he let her, he had the feeling she'd be his friend as well as his lover.

"Kevin…"

"No talking. Not now."

She nodded, but he caught the glimmer of disillusion in her eyes. But as he'd asked, there were no more words. No need for them. Their bodies spoke for them and with more meaning than anything they could say.

She wanted him. He felt it in her caress, heard it in the soft moans and contented sighs that escaped from her lips. Settling himself between her legs, he eased inside her bit by excruciating bit. She'd never know how difficult was his restraint.

He stroked a kiss across her lips, pausing to nibble and savor her sweet taste. As if to prove her words, she raised her hips a fraction, taking him ever deeper.

He groaned. Moist, warm, welcoming, and his. Kevin couldn't say which thought drove him over the edge, but with one thrust, he edged firmly inside. An expression of pure ecstasy covered her flushed face and he'd put it there.

"Kevin." Coming from her lips, his name sounded like the sweetest caress.

"Right here."

She sighed and whispered something that sounded suspiciously like "mine," before her muscles clenched around him. That's all it took. He hadn't realized he was so close to the edge, so ready to fall. He thrust in and eased out, each motion harder and deeper than the last. Caught up in the rhythm and beauty of Nikki, he came hard and fast. His climax not only caught him by surprise, but shook him to the depths of his soul.

Even as the aftershocks pulsed through him, Kevin knew he was in trouble. The only consolation he could find was knowing that Nikki was right there with him.

TWELVE

Married. Nikki rolled over expecting to find Kevin stretched out beside her, but her husband apparently had other ideas. She sat up in time to see him, fully dressed, attempting to slip from the bedroom. The disappearing act had eerie undertones of a night long past.

"Looking to avoid me?" she asked lightly, though she couldn't have felt more different.

He turned. Expecting to see guilt etched into his features, Nikki was relieved to see he merely looked like a man who'd gotten up earlier than his… wife. Since she was stumbling over the word, she hoped Kevin was having an easier transition to their newly married state. Of course last night had been spectacular, but then nights with Kevin always were. "I didn't realize you were awake."

"I wasn't till a minute or so ago."

"I thought so. You were out cold."

She smiled. "That's because you wore me out."

He stepped toward the bed, heat and desire unmistakable in his dark gaze. "I could say the same."

She glanced at the clock on the nightstand. "Then where are you off to so early?"

"To visit Max. His doctor checks in around ten A.M. and I want to make sure I'm there to hear everything. Otherwise I won't get near the truth."

The slight wrinkles around his eyes testified to the concern he felt for his father. Though he wouldn't admit it aloud, and perhaps he'd never admitted it to himself, he loved the older man. Nikki was certain.

She just wished he didn't have to beat his head into a brick wall every time he dealt with Max. But at least he wasn't alone anymore. She tossed the covers off and swung her legs over the bed. "Give me ten minutes and I'll go with you."

He stiffened. "No."

"I'll be quick. You'll be there by ten."

"You don't need to deal with Max and his addiction. I'll go alone."

Nikki narrowed her eyes. "At this point it's his health and he's your father."

"Right. Which makes him my problem. Besides I have a few stops to make first. I'll see you when I get home from work."

She folded her arms across her chest. "Whatever."

He walked toward where she sat on the bed and leaned down to brush a kiss over her mouth. He lingered, moistening her lips with his tongue and arousing her with the simplest touch.

She recognized his attempt at pacifying her, but he'd left her feeling more frustrated than placated. Still, when he lifted his head, she felt the loss.

"I know you mean well, but you don't need to be there for Max."

She'd have been there for him. But she wasn't surprised he didn't recognize the distinction. He may not feel she needed to be there, but she did.

Only after he left the house did she head for her old room downstairs to retrieve the information she'd accumulated from the local library. In her bag, she put literature she'd printed off the Internet and her stomach filled with a growing sense of dread. Kevin had problems letting her in—creating that sense of family and togetherness she needed, that her baby needed. Nikki had known that going in. But she'd also hoped he could learn to open up. Learn to love her.

But he was also the child of an alcoholic, and as she'd learned over the last few weeks, overcoming his past was a prerequisite to them having a future—and that was something he had to want to accomplish on his own.

Nikki wasn't averse to giving him a push in the right direction. All she could do then was hope for the best.

*   *   *

"He checked himself out."

Kevin glanced around the empty hospital room. Only the white rumpled sheets evidenced that Max had been there at all. "And you let him?"

The nurse who was assigned to Max's room shrugged. "He's an adult. We couldn't keep him if he didn't want to stay. Once the pain subsided, he wanted out."

Kevin groaned. He'd rearranged his schedule to meet with the doctor and Max, to make sure his father followed orders when he was released. The man needed to take care of himself and to cut out his drinking. Not a prayer of either one of those things happening, without…

"How is he?" Nikki's soft voice interrupted his train of thought.

Kevin turned to find her standing beside him. She'd pulled her hair back into a ponytail and wore a baggy striped shirt over black leggings. Ever since leaving the bar, she looked more like the girl he'd known, more like the woman he'd come to care too much about.

She placed a hand on his shoulder. "Where's Max?" she asked, glancing over his shoulder to the empty bed.

For the first time since he'd entered the patientless room, he was grateful Max had taken a hike. "Good question. Now I have one. What are you doing here? I thought you were home."

She opened her eyes wide, radiating innocence where he'd bet there was none.

"I was. I didn't know I needed your permission to leave the house."

"You don't. Unless you're coming here. And I specifically told you that you didn't need to concern yourself with my alcoholic father."

She nodded. "I know what you said. I never promised I'd stay away." She smiled, a wide grin that would have fooled anyone who didn't know her as well as Kevin.

Behind the bright smile lurked a hidden pain. He should have given in to her offer and let her come along with him, but he'd wanted Nikki protected from the likes of Max, his foul mouth and nasty temper. Drunk, he was mean enough—in pain and going through withdrawal, he was even worse. "I appreciate the thought but you don't have to be here."

"Families stick together," she said. "You might not realize that now but in time you will." She turned to the nurse. "Excuse me. What time did Mr. Manning leave?" she asked.

"As soon as the doctor came by and signed the discharge papers."

"Where is the doctor? I'd like to speak to him."

"He got called away on an emergency. Leave a message and he'll get back to you later."

"And Max?" Nikki asked again.

The nurse shrugged. "I assume you can find him at home. He said he had Jack waiting for him."

Kevin muttered a curse. Jack Daniels was his father's favorite weakness. "I need to find him." Kevin knew, even if his father didn't want to face it, that continued alcohol abuse could kill him.

"So let's go."

"I don't want you there," Kevin told her again.

She flinched as if he'd slapped her. Although he had no desire to hit her, he had no choice but to be harsh with her. Not only didn't he want her exposed to Max, but he didn't want her to see where he'd grown up. The old apartment, the revolting smells, the seedy neighborhood.

She straightened her shoulders. "Why? Why shouldn't I be with you when you're going through a rough time? Why shouldn't I help you take care of your father?"

"Because it's my job to do it. Alone. Just like it's

my job to protect you from my family. Such as it is," he muttered.

"Funny but I thought I was part of *your* family. Or is this..." She waved her ring in front of his face... "Is this a lie?"

"Of course it isn't. But there are parts of my family I intend to keep separate."

She let out a frustrated groan. "You know, life doesn't work that way. Family's family. You're lucky you have a father to take care of. I know he wasn't much of a parent growing up, but he's all you've got left now. Him and me. You don't seem too thrilled with him, so tell me. Are you trying to drive me away?" She shifted her bag onto her shoulder. "If so, you're doing a darn good job."

"Nikki, just back off and give me some space."

She shook her head sadly. "I've spent some time at the library, recently, to use the computer there and I Googled some research." She handed him a stack of papers and what appeared to be pamphlets.

He flipped through them, then turned the pamphlets face forward. "Alcoholics Anonymous and Al-Anon?"

"I thought Max might benefit from looking through the literature. You, too." Without another word, she turned and headed for the door.

Kevin wanted to stop her. With everything in him,

he wanted to call her back, to thank her.

To love her.

But glancing around the hospital room, and knowing what he had to deal with, he needed to do it alone. Protecting her was his number one priority and there was no way he'd let her around Max right then. In the future, if Max got his shit straight, he'd let Nikki near him, but not now. Not today.

* * *

With shaking hands, Nikki let herself into Janine's apartment. Her sister-in-law hadn't taken back the key, and she'd told Nikki to make herself at home any time she needed a friend. Nikki needed so much more than that now.

Life really knew how to dump on a person, she thought. On top of being rejected by Kevin, today was the day she and Janine would go through Tony's things. She brushed at the tears filling her eyes. She might have walked out on Kevin at the hospital, but he'd as much as thrown her out first.

If he couldn't let her into his life, let her help him through his pain, how could she expect to reach him? Ever? Instead of doing research for Max, she should have been looking into work options once the baby was born. Because Kevin had been making himself perfectly clear.

She just hadn't wanted to listen.

An hour later, Janine had returned and Nikki's thoughts shifted from Kevin to her brother. "Take a look at this." Janine walked out of the closet and held up a battered-looking high school football jacket in red and white, the old school colors.

"The things men hold onto," Nikki said with a laugh. Tony had worn that jacket every day for three years. "Ties to their youth."

"To look at in their old age. To show their grand-children." Without warning, Janine's voice cracked and she grabbed onto the wall for support.

Nikki jumped up and ran to her friend, walking her back to the bed and easing her down until she sat on the mattress. "I'm sorry," she said. "I wasn't thinking."

Janine shook her head. "It isn't you. It's me. It's this. It's life and how damn unfair it all is." She slammed her hand down on the bed in frustration.

Nikki raised her hand, wanting to offer comfort, then dropped it to her side. There was nothing she could give to Janine that would change the fact that Tony was gone. Nothing she could offer Kevin to change his self-perception. Nothing she could offer anyone, it seemed, but herself. And she hated the useless feeling that swamped her.

Once her sister-in-law had wiped at her eyes and blown her nose, Nikki turned toward her. "Do you want to put this off for a day or so?"

"No. It's not going to get any easier." She crumpled a tissue in her hand. "Would you mind making me a cup of tea?" she asked.

Nikki recognized the plea for privacy. "Sure." She placed a comforting hand on Janine's shoulder—whether or not her touch did any good, Nikki needed to offer *something* to her brother's wife. "I'll be right out there if you need me."

Janine nodded and Nikki headed into the other room. Making two cups of decaffeinated tea kept her busy and when the doorbell rang, she was grateful for yet another reprieve before having to face Janine's grief and the rest of her dead brother's things.

She glanced through the peephole. What she saw on the other side of the door wasn't a reprieve, but pain of another kind. She unlatched the lock and opened the door. "Hello, Kevin."

"Nikki." He gestured over her shoulder. "Can I come in?"

"It's not up to me. Janine's inside."

"She called the station and asked if they were finished with Tony's things. I'd stopped by to talk to O'Neill and the captain asked me to bring Tony's things over."

"You were at the station?" To her knowledge, he hadn't stepped foot in the place since giving his final statement after Tony's death.

"It's no big deal."

She disagreed, because much of Kevin's present dissatisfaction with life, in Nikki's opinion, stemmed from leaving a job he loved. One he was good at. One he'd walked away from thanks to the misguided notion that he was responsible for Tony's death. She'd thought he wasn't ready to deal with the past, but maybe she was wrong.

She glanced at the bag in his hand and sighed. Yet another thing for Janine to cope with. Nikki stepped back to let him pass. His masculine scent overpowered her senses, but not her reason. She hadn't forgotten Kevin's abrupt dismissal earlier or all it signified for their future.

Or lack of one.

"Whatever you say. Listen, Janine really isn't up to tackling Tony's work stuff right now. The bedroom's full of piles of things that the Salvation Army's supposed to pick up and she's really hurting."

"I don't doubt it." His eyes filled with compassion and emotion for Janine.

Nikki understood him enough to know he was also blaming himself for his role in her sister-in-law's pain. But she knew better than to reach out to him. She'd been slapped down before.

She grabbed for the bag Kevin carried and glanced

inside. Tony's uniform—the one he'd worn the night of the shooting—had finally been released by the police. "Can you take it home and I'll bring it back later in the week?" she asked, thinking of how upset Janine had been minutes earlier. "She can get to this last, after she's dealt with everything else."

He hesitated. "Are you sure?"

Nikki nodded. "She's a wreck in there."

"Okay then. I trust your judgment." He took the bag out of her hands.

"How's Max?" she asked, unable to help herself.

"Sober right now. But he's not in pain either, and that means he'll probably drink again."

She nodded. "Is he working?"

"He must be, because he has the money for alcohol. He's not getting it from me since I'm paying his rent directly to the landlord."

Enabling his father. Taking responsibility when it wasn't his to take. "Did you read the literature I gave you?" she asked.

"I appreciate the effort you made, but unless Max wants to be helped, there's nothing I can do."

She shrugged her shoulders. "Suit yourself." She didn't ask if *he* wanted to be helped. He'd have to come to that conclusion on his own. She'd obviously done all she could toward guiding Kevin in the right direction. Toward family. She couldn't make him take those final steps there.

She pointed toward the bedroom. "I really should get back to Janine."

"I can let myself out."

She turned and headed for the bedroom, unwilling to spend another moment looking into Kevin's dark eyes and wishing for things that couldn't be.

"I'll see you at home."

Nikki turned. Taking a deep breath, she drew on all her reserve strength. "Don't wait up," she said and shut the bedroom door behind her.

She had no intention of going back until after dark, after Kevin was in bed, after he'd gone to sleep. She couldn't handle him turning to her in bed. Not after he'd turned her out of his life.

*   *   *

Muffled voices sounded from the other room. Kevin paced the floor of Janine's apartment and wondered how the hell he'd managed to screw up the only good thing to happen to him in this lifetime.

Instead of leaving, he sat down on the couch. The papers Nikki had given him were bulky in his pocket, and he removed them, unfolding them and giving them a cursory glance. A substance abuse program was only as strong as the person joining it, and to date, Max had shown no inclination to sober up for good.

Despite himself, the literature was interesting reading. Leave it to Nikki to dig up information not only for the alcoholic, but for their families. He figured she was trying to tell him something.

Stretching out his feet, he glanced back toward the closed bedroom door. Tony was gone. Janine was on her way. Max wasn't a positive part of his life. Nikki was right—she was all he had left. He could work on keeping her there—or lose her for good.

The solitary life he'd chosen no longer held great appeal. Hell, most of his life no longer satisfied him. Three months ago he'd have said he didn't care whether or not he was happy as long as the people he cared about were safe; that had changed.

He hadn't drifted by the police station to talk to O'Neill because he'd referred him some clients. The telephone would have sufficed for that. Once again, Nikki was right. His trip there *was* a big deal. Kevin wanted more than eating, sleeping and breathing. He was coming out of the coma he'd been in since Tony was killed. Because of Nikki.

But he had a long way to go before he could thank her, or try to bring her completely into his life. He rose to his feet glancing back at the closed bedroom door. He realized he was taking a risk by continuing to shut her out, but the urge to protect her remained. Checking the address on the pamphlets, he folded the papers and shoved them into his back pocket.

But until he was certain he could offer her *everything* she wanted, everything she deserved, he was better off not getting her hopes up.

After all, hadn't he let her down before?

*   *   *

Nikki slipped into the house quietly and shut the door behind her. The silence told her she'd stalled long enough and Kevin was asleep. She just wished she and Janine had finished their painful task today, but there were more of Tony's things to go through. The lingering and the memories had taken up more time than they'd planned.

She tiptoed into the family room. For the first time since her marriage less than a week ago, she would sleep alone in her old bed. The notion chilled her and she hoped it wasn't a foreshadowing of her future.

She reached the middle of the floor when the room flooded with light. She let out a startled scream and jumped back, her heart pounding hard in her chest.

"I suppose I should be grateful you came home at all."

She pivoted toward Kevin's angry voice. "Of course I came home. I live here."

He leaned against the wall, looking forbidding and

furious. A muscle ticked in his jaw as he studied her through narrowed eyes. But her gaze was drawn to the rest of him, to the jeans that rode low on his hips and muscles rippling along his bare chest. She tried to swallow but her mouth had grown dry. She didn't stand a chance against him if she couldn't control her physical reactions.

"You could have called. Or didn't it occur to you that I'd be worried?" he asked.

"Of course it occurred to me. Protecting is your favorite pastime."

"You make it sound like that's a bad thing."

"Maybe because it is." Nikki drew a deep breath. She hadn't consciously planned an argument, but what did she expect when she'd deliberately stayed out until midnight? Perhaps they needed to clear the air, since she couldn't live with the pent-up anger any longer.

He stepped into the room. "Care to explain? I'm concerned about you and my child, and there's something wrong with that?" he asked. Then he took another step closer.

Nikki's breath caught in her throat. Anticipation and adrenaline flooded her veins. Yes, perhaps this argument was exactly what they needed for her to regain control of her senses and of her life.

She'd tiptoed around Kevin for too long. "What you feel is beyond concern. It's control."

His dark eyes glittered dangerously and she knew she was treading on sensitive ground. She'd never goaded him before, never pushed an argument to the point where he released his emotions. Apparently it was time for that, too.

"I don't want to control you, Nikki."

"You want to control situations. Same difference."

He grabbed her shoulders in a touch that, considering the emotions flowing between them, should have been rough but was exceedingly gentle. "I want to keep you safe."

She met his gaze head-on. "And you can't always guarantee that, even if you're by my side twenty-four hours a day!" She practically yelled in frustration. "You aren't responsible for fate."

"No, but I can make sure I'm there just in case." And then Kevin lowered his mouth to hers, forestalling any more arguing.

He was warm and she relished his touch, reveled in his scent. Although she couldn't turn him away, she wasn't ready to give in return. She didn't resist him; she needed the simplicity of the contact too much. And that's how he kept things between them—simple, as he nibbled and licked at the seam of her lips with his tongue. If he was intent on seducing her into submission, he was well on his way. Only the knowledge that he used sex to seduce himself into oblivion gave her the ability to remain strong. To think instead of cave.

And when she let him inside, for the first time, the intimacy nearly made her lose her resolve. Just a few more seconds, she promised herself, as his tongue swirled and tangled with hers. She gripped his forearms, her nails digging into his skin.

He exhaled a groan and slipped beneath her flowing shirt and dipped lower, to cup her behind and pull her tight against his rigid length. Liquid heat poured from her, sizzling fire burned in her veins. Why was this so perfect, when everything else between them was such a mess?

"Damn, but you feel good. Do you know what you do to me?" he muttered.

"Exactly because you do the same to me." She tipped her head backward forcing herself to look into his taut face, and forcing him to meet her gaze. His eyes were clouded with raw desire.

She could never resist him when he was like this, but tonight she had no choice. "Sex isn't the answer to our problems," she told him.

"We're here, we're together, and we're having a baby." His hand splayed over the light swell of her stomach.

His touch branded her. A silly, belated notion, considering he'd already done so by giving her his child.

"Forget any problems for now."

She shook her head, fighting his magnetic pull, fighting the lure of the future. "I wish I could." But if he couldn't give her anything besides great sex, they had no future.

She met his gaze, silently begging him with everything inside her to hear, and understand. "You can't base a lifetime on sex—no matter how good it is." And sex with Kevin was always good. Her heart beat loud and hard against her chest while her body throbbed in time to the steady rhythm, attesting to that particular truth.

He grabbed for her hand. "It's a start."

Was it her imagination or did his words sound like a plea for understanding? But she couldn't sleep with him and not have her emotional needs fulfilled, too.

"I thought so, too. But no more." She lifted her arms to his shoulders and pushed him away. He let her, backing off because she'd asked. Ironically, a part of her wished he'd press the issue and not allow her to withdraw so easily.

Her wish went unanswered and a chill washed over her as he placed emotional and physical distance between them.

"Go ahead. Get some sleep," he said in a rough voice. "It's late." He gestured toward her room—the guest room on the other side of the house. Far from his bedroom. Far from him.

She'd been hoping he'd understand everything she'd said tonight, and realized she'd been wishing for the impossible. Disappointment filled her— disappointment in him for his unwillingness to try and disappointment in herself for caring so much that he'd let her down.

She started for her room, and when she felt his burning gaze on her back, she turned around. "Kevin…"

"What?"

"I just want you to know I'll be out most of the day tomorrow. I'll be back sometime after dinner." She'd finally heard back from her guidance counselor. He had numerous options to discuss, and Nikki had convinced Janine to drive her back up to school to work out an arrangement that would enable her to graduate. Then maybe she'd find a private position that had some kind of day care.

She braced herself for the inevitable argument. Instead he merely shrugged his shoulders. "Suit yourself. You will anyway."

If she could close the distance between them, she'd do it in a heartbeat. But the next move wasn't hers to make.

THIRTEEN

Kevin pulled into the parking lot to Dr. Molloy's private office and shifted the gearshift to park. "This is standard?" he asked Nikki.

"For the fifth time, yes. It's my monthly appointment."

"And you're feeling okay?" He'd been so wrapped up in himself and Max lately that Nikki's health had taken a backseat.

"Perfectly fine. If I wasn't, you'd have heard about it. We live in the same house, after all."

But they barely communicated. Funny how he'd miss something he'd never really had. Nikki was sleeping beside him, but not with him. He sensed, in his gut, that the next move was his; but, damned if he knew how to make it or bridge the gap that was of his own making. He didn't let her into his life, so she didn't let him into her body. Somehow it didn't seem like a fair exchange.

"You ready?" he asked.

She nodded and minutes later, they were ushered into a small but modern-looking room. Immaculately clean and antiseptic-smelling, the examining room was a far cry from the dilapidated one downtown. And though Nikki got the same care from the same doctor, he couldn't help but be grateful she'd given in on this point and allowed him to foot the bill for private practice. At least he could feel like he was taking care of his family in a way that counted.

His family. Before he could process that thought, the door opened and Dr. Molloy entered.

She glanced at Nikki. "It's good to see you again, Nicole." Then she turned toward Kevin. "Mr. Manning. I'm glad to see you two have worked things out."

"I'd be foolish to turn down good medical care, Dr. Molloy." Nikki smiled, but Kevin wasn't fooled by her affable demeanor. As a general rule, she barely said two words to him without him prompting her first. This morning's "I have a doctor appointment at noon, remember?" was the longest sentence to pass from her lips.

He hadn't forgotten, but he was grateful she'd included him on her own. Otherwise he'd have to resort to caveman tactics again, and he didn't relish another scene in front of the good doctor.

"Well, I wasn't talking about using my private practice instead of the clinic," she said wryly. "But I think you made a wise decision. Now let's get started. Nikki, since this is a routine monthly visit, you don't need to undress. Just let me see that stomach and you'll be out of here before you know it."

Kevin watched as the doctor readied a small machine. With barely a glance in his direction, Nikki lifted her shirt to reveal her pale, rounded stomach.

He walked around to the side of the examining table and reached for her hand. Her protest was minimal—a slight resistant tug against his hand, but when he refused to release her, she stilled.

"Everything okay?" Dr. Molloy asked her. "Any unusual symptoms, questions?"

Nikki shook her head. "Everything's been fine lately."

"Nausea's gone?"

"Yes, thank goodness."

The doctor glanced at the chart. "You've gained two pounds. That's good considering you're merely putting back on what you lost during the first trimester." She shook a white bottle in her hand. "This might be cold," she warned, before squeezing the gel onto Nikki's exposed skin.

He watched, mesmerized by the sight of her flesh, by the knowledge that his baby lay growing inside her.

"Now I'm going to listen for this little guy's—or girl's—heartbeat. Ready?" she asked, then began rolling what appeared to be a rectangular-shaped instrument over the gel coating Nikki's stomach.

Without warning, a strong and steady sound reverberated throughout the room. "Hear that?" Dr. Molloy glanced up and met his gaze, a wide smile on her face.

He had the distinct sense that no matter how many times a day she heard the sound, Dr. Molloy got as big a kick out of the sound as her patients and their respective spouses. He listened in awe. Everything else in the room faded until only the combination of a whooshing noise and the distinct thump of his baby's heartbeat remained.

"That's… him?" Nikki asked, breaking into his concentration.

The doctor nodded. "Or her. Have you two discussed whether or not you want to know the baby's sex ahead of time?"

Sex. A boy or a girl. No longer an indistinct blur on a monitor screen, the whooshing sound confirmed what he already knew. They'd created a life. Together. Pride and many other emotions swelled in his chest and clogged his throat until he could barely swallow, let alone breathe.

"Knowing the baby's sex." Nikki's voice cracked as she spoke. "I don't know. We haven't talked about it." She rolled her head to the side and met his gaze. For the first time in two days, Nikki's emotions were raw and visible for him to see.

He understood because for perhaps the first time in his life, his were just as exposed. And he wasn't as uncomfortable as he'd imagined he'd be.

"What do you think, Kevin?" Nikki asked, obviously referring to the baby's sex.

He'd given a lot of thought to her accusations of control the other night and much as he'd have liked to turn a deaf ear, he couldn't ignore the truth. Or the fact that the controlling part of his nature was likely to drive her away and distance him from his child. He'd resolved to tread lightly or at least attempt to talk himself out of the burning need to hold the reins on everyone and everything around him.

The doctor had given him his first opportunity to back off and give Nikki space. Hoping to let her know he'd go along with whatever she wanted, he gave her hand a brief squeeze.

He glanced at Dr. Molloy. "Whatever Nikki wants is fine with me."

He didn't expect her to squeeze his hand back, or hang on even tighter, but she did. The lump in his throat grew larger. What he and Nikki shared, *could* share, was rare. He'd be a fool to lose it.

He'd truly be his father's son if he let it go without

a fight.

"Why don't you two give it some thought? It's not something I'll be finding out today anyway. Want to hear more or can I stop now?" she asked, with that same knowing grin. "You'll get to hear him every month."

"Or her," Nikki said.

Kevin raised an eyebrow. "Changing your mind? She thinks it's a boy," he said in response to Dr. Molloy's questioning look.

Nikki shook her head. "Just covering my bases."

The doctor lifted the machine and flipped the power off. She handed Nikki a towel. "Everything looks fine. You can clean up a bit and meet me in my office. I'll answer any other questions you have." With that, she slipped out the door.

Kevin and Nikki were alone. The sheen of tears in her eyes matched the emotion stirring inside him. "Do you have any other questions for her?" Kevin asked.

"Not right now." She crumpled a white paper sheet and wiped down her stomach, while he granted her the courtesy of turning away.

"Will you be okay if I put you in a cab and send you home? I need to run an important errand."

"Not a problem," she said, her words warring with the questions in her violet eyes.

No doubt she wondered why the man who professed not to want to let her out of his sight was suddenly willing to put her in a taxi alone. But she didn't ask where he was heading. And he didn't offer the information.

This short appointment had altered his entire life. To be more precise, Nikki had altered his life. But these last ten minutes had shown him what true bonding between people meant. For the first time, he understood some of what Nikki wanted from him— apart from the nights they used to share beneath the covers.

He heard the ripple of paper as she tossed the sheet into the trash and moved to his side. "As long as I'm in the city, I'd like to go to Janine's anyway."

"I can pick you up on my way home."

She shook her head. "No need. I don't know how long I'll be."

"It'll be too dark for you to take a cab... Never mind." Forcing himself to back off wasn't easy.

But words he'd read in Nikki's photocopied literature came back to haunt him. *Questions for adult children of alcoholics*, the paper had read. And Kevin had taken to reading them over at bedtime, when he was alone. He'd rather have been with Nikki, but she'd refused, citing his need to control and his inability to reach out to her. Questions he hadn't wanted to take seriously, but questions he couldn't ignore.

Did he anticipate problems when life was going smoothly? Did he isolate himself from other people? Did he have trouble with intimate relationships? Did he feel responsible for others, as he did for his drunken father? There were more, but those were the ones that stayed with him. Day after day, night after night.

He looked around him, at the room where he'd heard his baby's heartbeat for the first time. At the woman with whom he could share his life—if only he could learn how.

There was a way, he thought, recalling the literature once more. But he didn't know if he had it in him to take the steps he needed to take. He didn't know if he could ever stop blaming himself... for many things.

If he failed at this, he wanted to do it alone, if not in peace. But if he won, if he conquered this next demon, they both had a chance at a future.

"Kevin?"

He blinked at the sound of her voice. "What is it?"

"Thank you."

"For?"

"Being here. And letting me go." A soft smile curved at her lips.

He understood her, just as she understood him. And *that* was their start.

* * *

One by one, they filed out of the Al-Anon meeting room. Men and women looking just like him. Most held steady jobs. Some were married, others single. They looked like well-adjusted adults. But the one thing they had in common made Kevin question the last. They were all adult children of alcoholics.

He sat in his seat long after the others were gone, thinking about the most important things he'd heard here today.

He wasn't responsible for Max's alcoholism, nor his recovery. That much he'd known going in. He'd told Nikki the same thing when she'd asked him if he'd read the information she'd given him.

He shouldn't do things for Max that he could do for himself. In other words, he shouldn't be paying his rent when his father was an adult capable of holding down a job and earning money to pay the rent himself. If he chose to spend a paycheck on booze instead of necessities, that was his problem, not Kevin's. Yeah, like he could live with himself if his father got thrown out on the street.

But if he didn't stop aiding Max, Max's life would never be separate from his. And if he didn't get the lousy parts of Max's life out of his own, he didn't stand a chance with Nikki.

He glanced up to see the meeting leader standing in front of him.

"Glad to have you here," he said. "I hope you found us helpful."

Kevin heard the sound of his baby's heartbeat echoing inside his head. He saw Nikki's expectant face. He nodded at the man. "Helpful enough that I'll be back."

*   *   *

"Did you tell Kevin about your meeting at the college?" Janine asked.

Nikki folded the last sweater in her brother's closet and turned to face her sister-in-law. "No."

"Avoiding?" Janine asked in a teasing tone.

Nikki was grateful she could laugh in the midst of this chore. It made what was to come just a tiny bit easier. "You could say that."

Janine grinned. "I just did."

Nikki nodded. "Speaking of avoiding… Remember when we started this a few days ago?" She gestured to the bags and boxes scattered around the room.

"Like I could forget? Why?"

"Well, Kevin came by that day. And I told you he'd been by the station house and wanted to let you know they'd found a box of some of Tony's personal effects and they'd turn it over to you soon, remember?"

Janine grabbed for a pillow on the bed and hugged

it tight against her rounded stomach. "Go on."

"Well, they'd already done it. But I wanted it to be the last thing you dealt with, not the first. So the bag's in the living room. Along with his uniform from that night." She held her breath, waiting for Janine to yell at her for withholding something of Tony's or for making decisions she had no right to make.

Instead, she exhaled a long breath. "Thank you," she murmured softly. Her fingers curled tighter around the pillow until they were lost in the feather-like softness.

"So you're not angry?"

Janine shook her head. "I'm scared to even see his uniform. Last time I did, he was wearing it. And it was covered in..." Her eyes filled with tears and she swiped at them with the back of her hand.

Nikki's throat constricted and the pain in her chest was overwhelming. "Listen, we don't have to open the bag. We can put it aside and you can deal with it back home, or we can just..." She shrugged, unable to even suggest they throw out their last link to Tony.

"No. We'll go through it." Janine straightened her shoulders. "I have to do this. It's... closure, you know? Then I can go home and let the good memories take over." Tossing the pillow aside, she placed her hand over her stomach.

"You're sure you can handle this?" Nikki asked.

"Are you?"

She grabbed for Janine's free hand and clutched it inside of her own. "Hey, I'm as tough as you and don't ever forget it," she said, striving for a lightness neither of them felt.

Janine smiled. "Tony was proud of you, you know. If he never said it, it was because he was a big tough guy. But he loved you and he always knew you'd make something of yourself."

"So instead I got myself knocked up. Good thing he wasn't around to see it."

"Only because Kevin's face would be battered beyond recognition." Janine laughed. "Tony loved him like a brother, but for laying his hands on his baby sister… Then again, he married you, so all would be forgiven. And Kevin is officially part of the family now."

"Too bad he doesn't feel that way."

"Then *make* him feel it."

"Don't you think I've tried?" Nikki slammed her hand against the mattress. "He's like this fortress and the harder I try to get in, the more he shores up his defenses." And it hurt. She didn't know how many more times she could handle being rejected. "Besides he hasn't come to think of me as anything more than an obligation. Like you said, he did the right thing. Doesn't mean he's enjoying it."

Janine shook her head. "Tell him about school."

"What will that accomplish?"

"Maybe nothing. But maybe when he realizes you won't need him for long, it'll scare him out of that complacent shell of his and show him exactly what he has. And what he might lose."

Nikki rose from the bed. "You may have a point."

"I usually do. Now let's get this over with."

Not pretending to misunderstand, Nikki headed for the family room and returned with the bag Kevin had brought the week before. She placed it on the center of the bed while Janine stood off to the side, wide-eyed, staring at the sight as if it might come to life at any moment.

Nikki sighed. If her life ever got easy, she might not recognize her role in this universe. "Want me to open it?" she asked.

"Please."

Her hands shook as she untied the knot on the heavy plastic bag. Her breath caught as she pulled out the dark blue uniform her brother had worn for his last day on earth. And her heart constricted as she listened to Janine's soft cries as the blood stains on the material became apparent. She shut her eyes and tears fell anyway.

She wished Kevin were here to support her. Did he long for her presence when he put himself through a difficult task, like confronting his father? Or was he merely glad she was gone?

When Janine gingerly took the uniform out of her hands, Nikki stepped back. "Want me to give you some privacy?" she asked her sister-in-law.

"No. I really need your support. I need you."

"You've got me."

"You know it's not like I haven't accepted things."

"Hey, you're human. This isn't easy for me either, so don't be so hard on yourself. Have you given any thought to what you're going to do with it?" Nikki asked.

"Burn it," Janine muttered. "But I wanted to make sure I got all his personal things first."

While Janine patted down the clothes, searched through the pockets and looked through assorted pieces of paper, Nikki put the rest of the sweaters and other clothing into the last box. She turned back around to see Janine staring at a sheet of paper.

"What'd you find?"

"A report. A goddamn discipline report dated the day Tony died."

Nikki walked up beside her. "Mind if I take a look?"

Janine slammed the paper onto the bed and retreated, closing herself into the bathroom. Wondering what on that paper had Janine so upset, Nikki eased herself onto the mattress. She picked up the scrap of paper and turned it over.

"Failure to follow procedure. Not the first incident," she read aloud. Various other papers had scattered across the bed and each one she unwrapped contained another discipline report. Same complaint. Which didn't come as a surprise to Nikki, or Janine, she supposed, or anyone who knew her rebel brother well.

Including Kevin. But he'd chosen to shoulder the burden anyway, she thought, and was transported back to the night in Kevin's apartment.

The night Tony had died.

*   *   *

"It wasn't your fault," Nikki said.

Kevin grunted. "Tell that to your brother. I'm inside babysitting my drunken father and he gets an emergency call. Why take the time to go back inside for me?" he said, his voice full of self-loathing. A bottle of scotch sat on the kitchen table.

"Because it's procedure not to go out on a call without backup?" Nikki asked.

"I should have been in the goddamn car."

"And Tony shouldn't have gone off alone."

"If I hadn't been distracted, he wouldn't have."

She shook her head. Arguing with Kevin when he was in this mood wouldn't do either of them any good. "And you think

243

this is going to help?" she asked, lifting the half-empty bottle.

*"I'm no better than my old man and at least this proves it,"
he muttered. "And maybe if I finish it off, it'll help me forget."*

*She walked up beside him and held out her arms. "I'll help
you forget… if you'll do the same for me."*

*　　*　　*

The discipline reports proved what she'd known all
along. *It wasn't Kevin's fault.* Her renegade brother
wouldn't think twice about taking a call solo, especially
if Kevin was tied up with family. Family was important
to Tony, just as it was to Kevin. He just didn't realize
it yet. It was so like Tony to protect the people he
loved.

Just as it was like Kevin. Only that time, it had
backfired on her brother. He'd sabotaged his own life,
just like Kevin was slowly sabotaging his.

FOURTEEN

Kevin hit his father's doorstep first thing in the morning, hoping to find Max sober, or at worst, hungover. He stood in the hall banging on the door too long for Max to be inside having a morning cup of coffee. He groaned and steeled himself for the confrontation ahead.

The last confrontation, he hoped, until Max got his act together—or didn't. Kevin didn't want to think about the latter possibility. He reached into his pocket for a key just as the door swung open wide and Max greeted him in all his naked glory.

With a groan, Kevin pushed past Max and entered the apartment, pulling his father along with him. "Is that how you normally greet your neighbors?" Kevin asked.

"If they wake me then they get what they deserve."

"Well, go get some clothes on. I'll make a pot of

coffee."

"I don't need any."

Kevin raised an eyebrow. "Maybe not, but I do. Then I want to talk."

Max retreated, muttering something about an ungrateful and intrusive kid. The man never looked in a mirror, Kevin thought. He headed for the kitchen and dug out the coffee maker he'd purchased for Max years ago in the futile hope he'd actually make the stuff himself and aid in his own sobriety.

It took Max forever to pull on a pair of jeans and an old shirt, and by the time he sauntered back into the kitchen, Kevin had two cups of coffee ready and waiting.

"Have a seat, Dad. It's black. Just the way you like it."

Max threw himself into a chair.

"It's Monday. Don't you have to be at work?" Kevin asked, although he already knew the answer.

"I quit."

"More like you were fired," he muttered. He'd followed up on Max's last job and learned his father hadn't been a reliable employee. No big surprise there. "They needed someone who'd actually show up for work."

Max shrugged. "So now I have more free time."

"How are you going to pay your rent? Buy food?"

Buy alcohol, Kevin thought bitterly.

"You always come through for your old man."

Yes, he had. And he hadn't done either of them any good. But at least Max had just given him the opening he sought. "And why do you think I do that?" Kevin asked his father.

"Because I gave you life and you owe me," Max muttered. "Coffee tastes like mud."

"That's the cotton in your mouth from last night's binge. I do it because you're my father… and I love you." Once the words escaped his lips, Kevin realized it hadn't been as difficult as he'd anticipated.

Caught off guard, Max lowered the mug from his lips and it hit the table with a thud, sloshing liquid over the rim and onto the white Formica top. Kevin resisted the urge to wipe it up. It wasn't his mess.

"You're… I mean… you've been a good son," Max muttered, and Kevin understood how difficult even those words had been for his father.

The ones Kevin was about to say were even tougher because, though he didn't know it, he was about to give Max cause to rethink his opinion.

"Things have to change, Max."

"Yeah, yeah." Max yawned. "Are you through? I didn't get much sleep last night."

Kevin shook his head. "I'm not through. I'm going to be a father. You know what that means?"

"You weren't using protection?" Max said and laughed at his own bad joke.

"It means you're going to be a grandfather."

The rewording of the news seemed to take Max by surprise. He sat back in his seat and eyed Kevin in silence.

"I'd like you to be a better grandfather than you were a father, but that's up to you. Whether you see your grandchild or not, that's up to me." Kevin pushed his seat back and stood. "From here on in you're on your own. I'm not paying your rent and I'm not leaving food in the fridge."

"You've said that before. You'll always be there for your old man."

He shook his head. "Wrong. I never had anyone else relying on me before. Now I do." He had Nikki and he had a baby on the way. He'd do whatever it took to keep them in his life, even if it meant cutting Max out until he caught on to the concept of sobriety. Hell, at this point, even if he didn't have Nikki or the baby, *he'd* had enough. He wanted his life back.

"It's the end of the month and rent's due by the fifteenth. I suggest you call on your employer. I talked him into giving you one more shot if you want it. That choice is up to you."

"You don't mean that."

"Don't test me or you'll find yourself out on the

street." Kevin's heart thudded inside his chest. He knew the phone calls that would come, the pleas for money, the guilt because his father had no food in the refrigerator. He didn't know how he'd get through it.

Yes, he did. Nikki. If she hadn't washed her hands of him completely, she'd support him through this. And if she had, well, he'd see himself through. Either way, Max would sober up or Kevin was finished.

Max stood, shock rendering him mute. Kevin had never been this adamant before, and Max knew it. So did Kevin. Max also knew there were other people at stake now.

Knowing he had only one thing left to say, and knowing it was Max's only hope, he handed him the pamphlets and papers Nikki had given him on treatment programs for alcoholics. "Take this. Consider it my parting gift," Kevin said. "Read it and think about it. But don't call me or come looking for me unless you've cleaned up." Kevin started to leave, Max's curses and words following him out the door.

"Bring a kid into this world and look at the thanks I get. You'll remember this day when your kid turns its back on you."

He gripped the doorknob with sweaty palms. "With a lot of effort, I hope that won't happen."

"What goes around comes around, sonny. And remember, when you look in the mirror, you're just like me."

"That remains to be seen," Kevin muttered. He turned back once more. "You've got a family waiting—if you want one," he said to his father, then shut the door behind him.

Half an hour later, Kevin pulled up to the precinct. He might as well face all his demons at one time. If he wanted his job back, he had to ask.

But, first, he had to face why he'd walked out on it in the first place. Tony's death and fear. Fear of being responsible for and to another human being. A job as a security consultant left him responsible for property, something he could handle, though it left him cold and empty and unfulfilled.

He glanced at the black and white patrol cars lining the street. Was he ready to ride in one again? To back up a partner? To be responsible?

And remember, when you look in the mirror, you're just like me.

Kevin stepped out of the car. "I'm nothing like you, Max." And as he spoke the words, he knew for the first time that he spoke the truth.

The differences between Kevin and Max were more glaring than the similarities. While Max cared for nothing but himself and his next drink, Kevin was the opposite. If anything, he cared too much. Which was why he'd left a job he loved—because he'd failed his responsibilities and couldn't live with the fear that he was like Max, no good at caring for anyone but himself.

He'd live with Tony's death for the rest of his life, but he couldn't accept full responsibility any longer, nor could he let it run his life. Tony wouldn't have wanted him to eat, sleep and breathe guilt. Neither did those Tony had loved.

Like Nikki.

He loved her, but instead of showing her, he'd driven her away. All because he'd been too focused on his shortcomings and not on his potential. Because he'd been too busy trying to be responsible in a backward way that hurt, not helping everyone involved.

As he headed up the steps, Kevin shook off the memory of his father's bloodshot eyes as he spouted the Manning prophecy. He entered the precinct feeling lighter than he had in months, maybe years. Just believing in himself and the future made a huge difference in attitude.

Even if the future was more uncertain than ever.

*　　*　　*

The bathroom door opened wide and Janine walked out, eyes red and faced washed clean of makeup. Nikki understood. She was feeling pretty wiped out herself.

"Do you think Kevin knew Tony had been written up that many times? That he'd received the last one the same day he was killed?"

Nikki shrugged. "Did you know?"

Janine shook her head. "Nothing official. If you'd asked me, I could have guessed. I know he'd been orally reprimanded. The guys would joke about it over dinner. But it never bothered either one because Kevin had always backed Tony up and been able to anticipate his renegade moves."

"Riggs and Murtaugh," Nikki said laughing, recalling Mel Gibson and Danny Glover in the *Lethal Weapon* movies.

"It was funny," Janine agreed. "Until it got him killed. Why didn't he think of me before he ran off half-cocked?" Janine rubbed her hands over her eyes.

Nikki nodded, barely able to draw a breath, let alone formulate a response. "I don't know the answer to that any more than I understand why Kevin still blames himself for that night."

"Well, we're finished here," Janine said. "The Salvation Army will be here in an hour for the rest of the things, the landlord rented the apartment with most of the furnishings…"

"And you want to be alone." It wasn't a difficult guess. "Since your flight is tomorrow night, can I see you to say good-bye?"

Janine nodded. "Kevin invited me to come by."

"Of course he did." He just hadn't mentioned it to her. She fingered the paper in her hand and gestured to the rest of the papers unraveled on the bed. "Do you mind if I take these?"

"Not at all. You want to show them to Kevin?"

"Yeah," she whispered. "I do." She didn't think it would change anything, but he deserved to know. Deserved to be relieved of one huge responsibility with which he'd saddled himself.

And after, she'd let him know she planned to finish school and find a job, maybe he'd be twice as relieved. Because soon after, he could be relieved of her as well.

*   *   *

Kevin sat on the couch, listening to the sounds of the night. He wasn't surprised Nikki had chosen to stay late at Janine's. It seemed to be a habit with her these days, without calling or without texting, and then her crawling into their bed after she thought he was asleep. But not tonight.

Tonight, she needed to listen to what he had to say. To know he was making an effort to do as she asked and give her the family she wanted, by learning how to separate himself from his past. Opening himself up to her wouldn't be easy. He wasn't sure he was prepared. But by the time she walked into the house, he was ready.

"Hi." She put her keys onto a small table and looked at him, questions in her eyes. "What are you doing up?"

"Waiting for you."

"Oh." She bit down on her lower lip. "How come?"

"I wanted to talk." He patted the cushion beside him. "Have a seat?"

She nodded. "Because I needed to talk to you, too." She sat down beside him. The scent he'd come to associate with Nikki—with this house—permeated the air, wrapped around him.

Without prompting, she drew closer and rested her head on his shoulder. She felt good—beyond sexually arousing him, she lifted his spirits and lightened the burden that was his life.

For that, he owed her. "You said you wanted to talk. Ladies first."

She didn't argue the point, another odd sign. Instead, she pushed herself away, setting distance between them. Distance he hadn't wanted.

She curled her legs beneath her so that her baggy shirt draped over her knees. "It's about the night Tony was killed."

All the air left his lungs in a mad rush, while everything inside him froze. Not that he'd put it behind him. He lived with the reality every day of his life. Just looking into Nikki's eyes on a daily basis reminded him of his failures, and his similarities to his father. He could change his reactions to his father's behavior, but he couldn't change heredity.

"Could you replay that night for me?" she asked. "Please?"

He'd relived that night to the department's satisfaction only because he, too, had violated procedure by checking on Max while on duty, and because he wanted official closure on Tony's death. But he hadn't opened up for the shrink his boss had suggested he see, nor did he want to start now. His nightmares and daily living were enough of a replay for him.

"I wouldn't ask if it wasn't important," she said.

This was Nikki asking him to open up and hadn't he just said he owed her? He had no choice but to give her what she asked for. "We were on duty, but it was quiet. And for a change I needed to pick up after Max."

Silence pulsed thick around them. She obviously respected his need to do this his way. But as he spoke, all the responsibility and guilt he'd been trying to let go came flooding back. "I was violating procedure, but neither of us mentioned it. Tony understood. He knew all about Max."

Which was more than Nikki could say, she thought. Until he'd had no choice but to enlighten her, she knew nothing about his alcoholic parent or his childhood. To be fair though, she shouldn't have expected him to open up to her. He hadn't shared her dreams of happily ever after, even after forever had been thrust upon him.

"Max's landlord had called. He hadn't seen him in over twenty-four hours, and with Max, silence is as much trouble as his harassment. I went inside, alone, while Tony waited in the car." He clenched and unclenched his fists. "It was supposed to be a quick check. My radio relayed a nine-one-one call and I ran for the car. Tony was supposed to wait."

"But he didn't."

"No. I came outside and he was gone. By the time I caught up with him…"

He didn't have to finish his sentence. They both knew how it ended. "And you blame yourself."

"Of course. I had no business being with Max while I was on duty. Add to that, I should have known that if Tony got a call, he'd take off—with me or without me."

Bingo, Nikki thought. "So it's your fault my brother was a renegade cop?"

"It's my fault I wasn't there to back him up. The reason Tony and I worked so well together was because we anticipated each other's every move. I was always able to second-guess him before he got himself in trouble. Until I was distracted by Max."

"So you think you blew it. Let Tony down."

He nodded. "I let all of you down. Tony, you, Janine—in the worst possible way. I let myself get distracted and I didn't take care of what counted. I proved my father's prophecy right… What the hell are we talking about this for?" he asked suddenly.

Before he could jump from the couch, Nikki grabbed for his hand. "What prophecy?" she asked.

"It's nothing."

"I think it's something or else you wouldn't be carrying it around with you. So spill."

Kevin met her gaze with a steely one of his own. "When did you become a bossy thing?" he asked.

"I've always been one. You just haven't paid attention. Now answer the question."

"Max believes Mannings aren't good at taking care of anyone but themselves."

She'd heard that before and rolled her eyes.

"It's true in his case, and haven't I been proving that lately? First Tony, then sleeping with you, getting you pregnant…"

She blinked, stunned by his logic and hurt by his words. Although she realized he hadn't meant to wound her, he certainly had.

He'd also given her a perfect opening for both things she had to say. "Well, I can relieve you of some of that misplaced guilt. Janine was going through Tony's personal effects from work. Did you know he'd been officially reprimanded many times for failure to follow procedure?" She reached into her bag and pulled out the stack of papers. "The latest one was given on the morning of the day he was killed."

He folded his arms over his chest. "I wasn't privy to anything in his private files."

She waved the papers in front of his face, frustrated that she hadn't cracked the stoic but self-deprecating façade he presented. "Don't you understand what these mean? *They absolve you of responsibility.* Tony was my brother and I loved him, but he was a loose cannon and responsible for his own death. You two chose to stop by Max's together, but he chose to go off without you."

She placed the papers in his lap. "There's one more thing," she said, when he remained silent. "I went to speak to my advisor at the university," she told him. "There's no way I can complete my student teaching next year. My November due date won't allow me to do it in the fall, and for the first six months I don't intend to leave the baby, so the spring's shot."

Because her child's welfare was of paramount importance, she'd come to terms with the fact that she'd have to rely on Kevin's good will and financial support. No matter that she didn't want to burden him with a marriage that wasn't working, she forced herself to accept that he'd helped place her in this position, so she had no choice but to accept his help for his child.

He leaned closer. "I wasn't aware you were considering going back to school. I think…"

She didn't want to hear his opinion on her decisions. "Just hear me out. My advisor's given me a reference. I'm going to do tutoring at some of the local elementary schools and then I plan to apply for a part-time job starting next January, when the baby's a few months old. That way, I can keep the baby with me and still work…"

"Whoa." He held up his hand. "What's all this about? I thought you planned on taking it easy until the baby was born."

She raised an eyebrow. "Really? When did I say that? I hadn't planned on taking it easy at all, until the baby's welfare was at stake. So I quit and we got married, all for the same reasons. But when did I ever say I'd take it easy? As a matter of fact, when did I ever discuss my future plans with you at all?"

"You didn't."

But she'd wanted to. Beyond making love, though, there hadn't been all that many times when they'd relaxed enough for her to open up with *her* dreams.

"But you wanted to. You still do."

She folded her arms over her own chest and met his gaze. "Yes, I did. I do." Nikki held her breath. She'd thrown down the gauntlet. All that remained was for him to take—or reject it.

Silence greeted her. Nikki was done with this conversation. She'd opened herself up and gave him the perfect opportunity to ask her about her dreams, her thoughts and yet he said nothing.

She rose to her feet "I can't do this anymore. I can't lie in that bed and pretend to be your wife. I can't make love to you knowing that during the day that connection between us crumbles because you let it. Sex just isn't enough to base a lifetime on." Her hands shook but she had no pockets in which to shove her fists, no means of hiding her trembling. Or pain.

He stood up beside her. "You're leaving me?"

She shook her head. "I wouldn't do that. I married you, for better or for worse. You gave our baby a name, you gave me the money to provide our child with a decent start in life. I owe you for that."

"I don't want your loyalty."

"And I don't want to be just an obligation to you, but we don't always get what we want, do we?" Shaking off the pain, at least the pain that showed, Nikki forced her voice to remain steady. "I think it's best if I move back to my old room."

*   *   *

Kevin shouldn't have let her move into her old room but he needed to think over what she said. Not long, just enough time to process the fact that she'd been planning a whole future without including him… and he'd driven her to it. Now he lay alone in his bed. He had slept by himself for over thirty years and this was the first time he'd truly felt alone. Nikki hadn't just gone to sleep in a separate room; she'd taken steps to create a life separate from his. He wasn't a fool. Necessity had been the only thing that had brought her into his life and into his home. Given a choice, she'd still be in school. Given a choice, she wouldn't be saddled with his child.

So he wasn't surprised she'd planned ahead. That streak of independence and ability to survive had served her well once before. It was just one of her many traits he admired, one of the many facets of Nikki that attracted him.

Yet the very traits he admired, were the ones destined to draw her away, if he allowed it. He wouldn't. He'd give Nikki a bit of time to cool down, let her have some space. He'd give her some time just like she gave him. But soon, he was getting her back in his bed where she belonged.

*   *   *

"And you'll keep in touch."

Kevin watched as Nikki hugged Janine. In her voice and her gestures, he could feel her reluctance to let go. Janine was her last link to Tony and probably the one person who didn't make her feel so alone.

"You know I will. And once we've had these kids, and as soon as you can travel, I expect that husband of yours to bring you all out west to visit." Janine's gaze met his.

"I think I can handle that," he said wryly.

Nikki turned, tears in her eyes. "You know I'm going to hold you to that promise," she told him.

He nodded. At least that was one promise he knew he could keep.

Janine glanced at Nikki. "Can I have a word alone with Kevin?" she asked. "It's not that you…"

"You don't have to explain," Nikki said. "I'll be in my room when you're done. Don't you dare leave without a last good-bye."

When she'd walked out of the room and the sound of footsteps on the hardwood floor trailed off, Janine glanced over. "Want to sit?"

"Might as well. I always do better sitting when I'm being lectured," he said with a grin. He hadn't realized how much he would miss Janine until this moment. "I'm going to be lost without you telling me what to do."

She lowered herself into one of the kitchen chairs and he sat beside her. "That is such a line. But I'll miss you, too."

Resting his chin on his hands, he met her gaze. "You really don't blame me, do you?"

She shook her head. "I never did. But I will blame you if you screw this marriage up. Don't you know a good thing when you see it?" she asked. She grabbed for his hand and clasped it tight. "Life's too short to waste a minute of it. I don't care how old or tired that cliché is, look at me and Tony and you'll know it's true."

He squeezed her hand back. "It shouldn't have happened," he said, thinking of Tony.

"No, but it did. Learn from it," she urged him.

He planned to. "Take care of yourself and that baby you're carrying. And if you need anything, and I mean anything, you pick up the phone. Okay?"

She nodded, then rose to her feet and grabbed him in a hug made awkward by the size of her stomach. Nikki would be that big one day soon and he wanted the right to hug her anytime he pleased. The thought came to him out of the blue, and remained.

"You're one of the good guys, Kevin. It's time you realized that."

* * *

She was alone. Janine's car pulled out of the driveway. Nikki hugged her arms to her chest and blinked back tears. Then with a resolve she'd dredged up too many times this past year, she shook off the melancholy that threatened. She wasn't alone; she had herself and her baby. Two very good reasons to push forward and go on. Janine, herself, was an inspiration there.

As Nikki sat on the front stoop, counting her blessings, she decided it was time to do more than think in the abstract—it was time to plan for this baby. Pushing herself to her feet, she headed inside. The sound of the television blared from the living room. She avoided Kevin and circled behind him to enter the kitchen.

Phone book on the table, pad and pen in hand, she made a list of all the things she'd need when the baby was born and rough estimates of what it would cost.

"What are you doing?"

At the sound of Kevin's voice, she jumped in her seat. She resisted the urge to hide her lists. "Baby planning."

"Mind if I take a look?"

She shook her head. He pulled up a chair beside her and straddled the back. She watched as his gaze flickered over the list. With his dark head bent forward, she could look all she wanted without being caught staring. The longing in her heart was frightening in its intensity.

He raised his gaze. "Not that I've been baby shopping lately, but some of these prices look a little low to me."

"They're rough estimates," she murmured. Of used furniture. Not that she had any intention of sharing the details with him.

"What do you say we go check out the real thing?"

She blinked, startled by his suggestion and frightened by the hope one tiny suggestion generated. "I don't think that's necessary."

He shrugged. "I do." He turned the yellow pages around to face him.

Minutes later, he'd added a list of stores and addresses to her list of items. None of the names on his list matched the ones she'd mentally compiled in her head. Top-of-the-line stores, they'd contain all the things she'd love for her child to have.

But she wouldn't have a prayer of paying Kevin back for years to come. "You know, I'm exhausted."

His dark gaze met hers. As usual, she was drawn into the compelling depths. "It's no wonder you're beat. Saying good-bye to Janine wasn't easy."

"For you either."

He covered her hand with his larger, stronger one. "You're not alone, Nikki."

She wanted to believe him. And that was the scariest thought of all. "I think I'll lay down," she said, desperate to escape from his magnetic pull and her own unrequited desires.

"Good idea. Rest up today and after work tomorrow, we'll start with the first store on the list."

His tone of voice didn't leave room for argument, but that wasn't the main reason she didn't fight his intentions. As a general rule, she had a difficult time reading his cloudy gaze, but his eyes were clear, his expression lighter than usual. He was looking forward to shopping for their baby.

Nikki couldn't deny him the pleasure. Worse, she didn't want to. *You're a fool, Nicole.*

Because she loved him.

FIFTEEN

Weeding wasn't a pretty chore, but it was a productive task and the improvement was always evident. Nikki needed to see improvement in *something*, even if it wasn't in any particular area of her life. If she kept at it long enough, maybe it would be too late for her to shower and change and still have time to hit the baby stores with Kevin later tonight.

She didn't know if she could handle it. A mother and father shopping for their unborn baby was supposed to be a joyful occasion, one that was fun and full of hope and promise. But all she would feel this evening was the pain of what would never be.

"Hey you, keep that up and you'll be pulling the azaleas along with the weeds."

At the sound of Kevin's voice, she glanced up but was blinded by the late afternoon sun. "I was just gardening."

He knelt down beside her. "Looks like you were hacking up the flowers to me."

She shrugged. "It keeps me busy."

He settled himself beside her, looking comfortable in the soft green grass. "And that's important to you? Keeping busy?"

She nodded. "It stops me from dwelling on things I can't change." And sometimes it gave her time to dwell on those same things and attempt to come to terms with herself and her life.

"Do you miss school?"

"I don't miss being in school. I wish I had finished before… Well, let's just say I wish I was more self-sufficient."

He leaned forward. "I'm sorry relying on me's so hard."

She sighed. "It isn't you. It's the taking I hate. It's not like this is a real marriage and we planned for this baby and decided I'd be a stay-at-home mom."

"What if it were a real marriage? What if every-thing was exactly the way you wanted it to be? Would you get your degree and go back to work or would you stay at home with your kids?"

She narrowed her gaze. This was the most serious conversation they'd had since… well, ever. And he'd initiated it. She was curious to see where it led.

She leaned back in the grass, resting on her palms.

"I'm not sure if I should answer. You'll think I'm awfully old-fashioned."

"I already *know* you're hopelessly old-fashioned." He laughed, a rich, vibrant sound she'd never heard before.

Hope, something she'd have sworn she no longer believed in, came springing back to life. Nikki quickly tamped it down. Just because Kevin was making small talk didn't mean she should start weaving fantasies of forever-afters.

"Well?" he prodded.

"I'd get my degree—to have it—for me. It's only one semester, after all. But then I'd stay home. I want my kids to have security and a mom that's around. And I know I'd be just as fulfilled being home with my kids as I would teaching someone else's. More so, really."

He grinned. "That's what I thought. And that was the easy question," he said, sobering. "I have a tougher one."

She shrugged. "Go for it." She might as well humor him because he seemed comfortable and relaxed and she didn't think he'd be leaving any time soon. Plus the longer he talked, the less time they'd have for shopping later.

"What do you want?"

Her fingers curled into the grass. "What?"

"What do you want? From life, from marriage…

from me."

He'd gone too far. She couldn't humor him. Not anymore. Not at her own expense. Shopping for the baby was preferable to this. "Obviously you're in a good mood, Kevin, but excuse me if I don't want to play along." She started to rise, but her growing stomach made a quick exit impossible and her sudden move resulted in a pulling pain in her right side. With a groan, she pulled her knees up to ease the sudden cramp.

"Hey, are you okay?"

She nodded. "I'm used to it. Sometimes I wake up in the middle of the night and stretch and I end up feeling like I pulled a muscle I didn't even know I had."

"I didn't know that," he said, sounding very upset that he had been left out.

She didn't understand him today. "There's no reason you should."

"There's every reason. Nikki, I…"

She leaned forward until she was too close to his handsome face. Too close to his arousing scent and the warmth of his skin. "You… what?"

"Love you. I love you."

Her breath left in a whoosh and the pain she'd experienced suddenly returned, but this time too close to her heart. "Don't say what you don't mean." She couldn't handle it. Tears welled in her eyes and she swiped at them with the back of her hand. "Hormones," she muttered.

He reached forward and rubbed at the tip of her nose. "Dirt," he said.

She laughed, though she wasn't feeling anything that resembled humor.

*   *   *

Kevin held his breath. Laughter and joking around was good, but not when he'd put his heart on the line. He'd told her he loved her and she was staring at him in shock.

"You don't believe me." He wasn't certain what she was feeling, but he knew for a fact she wasn't taking him seriously.

How could he blame her when he'd never given her any indication of his feelings? Never even tried.

Tears streamed openly down her dirt-streaked face, yet she'd never looked more beautiful to him. He felt as if he were seeing her for the first time. Through his new perspective, perhaps he was.

He felt his future slipping away. He reached out and placed his hand over her rounded stomach. "Have you felt the baby kick yet?" he asked.

She shook her head then obviously changed her mind and nodded. "Sort of. Little butterfly flutters."

"Can I feel?"

"It's too soon to feel it from the outside. Why are you doing this?"

"Because it's past time. And I don't want to lose you. Have I?" He needed the answer as much as he feared it. Probably more.

"You do know how to drop a bombshell," she muttered. "You *love* me?"

"Enough to take a look at myself through your eyes. Enough to walk into one of those Al-Anon meetings. Twice. Enough to lay down the law with Max. I told him he has family waiting but only if he sobers up. Otherwise he's completely on his own." His gut clenched with guilt again. "I can get through it, but it would be so much easier if I wasn't alone. Did I jump the gun telling Max he had *us* waiting?"

"Is this another 'I'll give it my best shot at being a family'?" she asked, her voice shaking.

He spread his hands out in front of him. "Think about everything I just said. Does it sound like an I'll try or like I've already done it?" he asked. "I didn't even think of coming to you before I'd taken all the first steps on my own." And he'd risked waiting too long and losing her in the process.

He heaved a groan. "There's nothing else I can say. The rest is up to you."

He wondered if his heart had ever beat so fast or

so loud. As he sat waiting, he got an inkling as to what he'd put Nikki through these past months. *If*, as Janine believed, she loved him.

"The first time I met you, I thought I fell in love. At first sight, if you can believe that." She glanced down as she spoke. "Later, I chalked it up to a crush. I had to, since you never spared me a second glance. Until that night."

"When everything changed."

She nodded. "I didn't come to your apartment for that, but I didn't wake up with regrets, either. If anything, I woke up with a sense of hope despite the fact that I'd just lost my brother. I thought, no, I really believed I had a chance. That *we* had a chance."

"And then I took off."

"And reality set in. It's taken months, but you finally convinced me—you couldn't come around, couldn't be part of a family. And now..." She pounded the grass in frustration. "I can't read you, I don't understand you, and I'm afraid if I let myself believe, I'm setting myself up for more pain."

And that pain was more than evident, in her eyes and in her drawn expression. In the recent past, as recent as yesterday, he'd have agreed with her and walked away. But no more.

He reached for her, grasping her shoulders and turning her to face him. "I can't do any more than promise, and remind you that the things I've said to you today, I've never been able to say to you bef—" He didn't get to finish.

Nikki threw herself into his arms, pushing him backward onto the grass.

"So this means… what exactly?" he asked once he'd caught his breath.

"I love you, too. I always have. Those dreams never died; they just got a little tarnished, you know?"

He brushed long strands of hair out of her face. "I thought I drove you away for good."

"I never went far. Not really. And as for Max, I'm the one who told you we were a family."

At the mention of his father's name, he exhaled a long groan. "I nearly went back to his apartment about ten times today."

"I can't even begin to imagine how hard it was, but you did the right thing. And I'll be there for you every step of the way."

"I always knew that, in here." He pointed to his heart. "But in my head, I knew I'd tested you too many times to deserve forgiveness."

She rested her body on top of his. For the first time in awhile, he felt her heat and her curves flush against him. The swell of her fuller breasts and the curve of her stomach pressed into him. He wrapped his arms around her waist. "You feel good," he whispered in her ear.

She let out a contented moan. "You feel even bet-ter."

"I can promise you I love you and that I'm here to stay, but I can't promise I won't need some guidance on this emotional give-and-take business."

She brushed a kiss over his lips. "Oh, I think I can guide you. You just need to have an open mind."

"My mind is open… to lots of things."

She grinned. "Why don't you tell me what you have in mind."

He rolled to his side, taking her with him. "I could spend the rest of the night telling you what I have in mind."

"What about furniture shopping."

He held her in his arms, grateful for a second chance. "I think that can wait. After all, neither of us is going anywhere."

She smiled. "Not for a long, long time."

EPILOGUE

The now-familiar sound of the baby's heartbeat sounded in the small examining room. Nikki felt the rush of warmth fill her body; and, when Kevin squeezed her hand, she also felt it in her heart.

Dr. Molloy moved her instrument over the gel coating her stomach. "Have you two decided on whether you're ready to know the sex?" she asked.

Nikki's stomach leapt in anticipation. They'd discussed the possibility last night into the late hours of the morning. Talking and bonding with Kevin had been almost more moving than making love.

Almost. Because nothing could compete with the sensation of joining their bodies together and *knowing* that bond transcended the physical. And always would.

"We want to know," Nikki said.

Kevin cleared his throat "Are you sure? Because there's no going back. Once we know, there's no surprise."

"I'm sure. For a number of reasons." Once they knew the sex, they'd know the name and then the bonding process could begin even stronger pre-birth. "Are *you* sure?" she asked him.

"Absolutely." His grip on her hand became stronger.

"Okay then, let's see if this little guy—or girl—is willing to cooperate." The doctor moved the instrument around her stomach. "Sometimes they get shy. They lie on their side, or they cross their legs."

Nikki laughed. "That would figure."

"A-ha. Here we go." Her hand movements stilled and both Nikki and Kevin stared at the monitor. "Now remember, this isn't foolproof."

"How's your record running, Doc?" Kevin asked.

"Well I don't want to brag, but I haven't been wrong yet."

He chuckled. "I'll take those odds. How about you, Princess?"

These days, that name made Nikki feel safe and cherished. "I'm dying here. Would you two stop stalling?"

"Want to take a guess first?" the doctor asked.

"Girl," Kevin said. "With violet eyes and dark hair."

"Boy," Nikki disagreed, recalling how certain she'd

been for so long. Then sudden doubt assailed her. "Make that a girl."

At Kevin's raised eyebrows and quizzical look, Nikki shrugged. "It's a woman's prerogative to change her mind. Especially a pregnant woman."

"Okay, Doc. Let's hear it."

"It seems that Kevin's right." The doctor moved the instrument in small circles. "And so are you," she said to Nikki.

"So it's a girl," Nikki said, envisioning pink and lace and eyelet and Kevin's dark hair, and his deep, dark eyes.

"Yes. It's also a boy."

"Impossible unless we're talking mutant," Kevin said, obviously misunderstanding.

Nikki didn't blame him. She wasn't sure she wanted to accept the truth either. "You're joking, right? You do this to every set of nervous parents. We can't possibly be having twins."

"Twins?" Kevin sounded as if he were gasping for air.

"I might not be able to predict the sex, but I can definitely predict the number," Dr. Molloy assured her.

"Oh God." Nikki said, surprised.

"Two babies?" he asked.

"Three, counting you," Nikki said, laughter in her

voice.

"I think I'll give you two a few minutes alone to digest this information." The doctor cleaned up and walked out of the room.

After Kevin helped her to a sitting position, Nikki got a good look at his face for the first time. He was pale, and she couldn't read his expression beyond the fact that he was obviously stunned.

"Think you can handle it?" she asked, suddenly worried that after all their efforts at making things work between them, he'd be overwhelmed enough to back off again, due to the thought of two unexpected bundles instead of the one they'd known about.

He shook his head. She hoped he was clearing his thoughts, not answering no. "Kevin?"

"I'm... fine. I think," But he grinned then, and Nikki relaxed. As much as she could with the new-found knowledge hanging over her head.

He grabbed her hand. "It's overwhelming," he admitted. "But exciting, too. We'll handle it together."

Together. She liked the sound of that word. "Do you want to call Max and tell him?" Nikki asked.

Kevin's father had been admitted to the hospital again a few weeks back and had willingly gone into a rehabilitation center after that. Although Kevin was footing the bills, it would be worth it if he got his father back in his life again.

He shook his head. "He doesn't need any more pressure. Besides, I'd like to take the time to adjust to this alone with you."

She looped her arms around his neck. "Alone. I like the sound of that."

"It's something we should take advantage of now because there won't be much more solitary time in our lives."

"No. And I'm grateful for that."

"Me, too. And I'm grateful for you."

Did you enjoy this sexy stand-alone novel? If so don't miss these stand-alone titles:

The Right Choice

Suddenly Love

Perfect Partners

Unexpected Chances

Worthy of Love

Thank you for reading **WORTHY OF LOVE**. I would appreciate it if you would help others enjoy this book too. Please recommend to others and leave a review.

Meet the Dares!
Dare to Love – Book 1 Dare to Love Series –
(Ian Dare)

Keep up with Carly and her upcoming books:

Website:
www.carlyphillips.com

Sign up for Carly's Newsletter:
www.carlyphillips.com/newsletter-sign-up

Carly on Facebook:
www.facebook.com/CarlyPhillipsFanPage

Carly on Twitter:
www.twitter.com/carlyphillips

Hang out at Carly's Corner! (Hot guys & giveaways!)
smarturl.it/CarlysCornerFB

CARLY'S MONTHLY CONTEST!

Visit: www.carlyphillips.com/newsletter-sign-up and enter for a chance to win the prize of the month! You'll also automatically be added to her newsletter list so you can keep up on the newest releases!

Dare to Love Series Reading Order:
Book 1: Dare to Love (Ian & Riley)

Book 2: Dare to Desire (Alex & Madison)

Book 3: Dare to Touch (Olivia & Dylan)

Book 4: Dare to Hold (Scott & Meg)

Book 5: Dare to Rock (Avery & Grey)

Book 6: Dare to Take (Tyler & Ella)

*each book can stand alone for your reading enjoyment

DARE NY Series (NY Dare Cousins) Reading Order:
Book 1: Dare to Surrender (Gabe & Isabelle)

Book 2: Dare to Submit (Decklan & Amanda)

Book 3: Dare to Seduce (Max & Lucy)

*The NY books are more erotic/hotter books

Read on for an excerpt of **Dare to Love,**
Ian and Riley's story.

Dare to Love
Excerpt

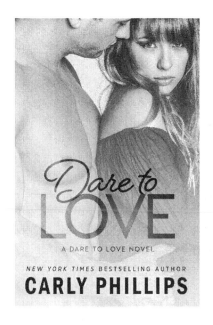

Chapter One

O nce a year, the Dare siblings gathered at the Club Meridian Ballroom in South Florida to celebrate the birthday of the father many of them despised. Ian Dare raised his glass filled with Glenlivet and took a sip, letting the slow burn of fine scotch work its way down his throat and into his system. He'd need another before he fully relaxed.

"Hi, big brother." His sister Olivia strode up to him and nudged him with her elbow.

"Watch the drink," he said, wrapping his free arm around her shoulders for an affectionate hug. "Hi, Olivia."

She returned the gesture with a quick kiss on his cheek. "It's nice of you to be here."

He shrugged. "I'm here for Avery and for you. Although why you two forgave him—"

"Uh-uh. Not here." She wagged a finger in front of

his face. "If I have to put on a dress, we're going to act civilized."

Ian stepped back and took in his twenty-four-year-old sister for the first time. Wearing a gold gown, her dark hair up in a chic twist, it was hard to believe she was the same bane of his existence who'd chased after him and his friends until they relented and let her play ball with them.

"You look gorgeous," he said to her.

She grinned. "You have to say that."

"I don't. And I mean it. I'll have to beat men off with sticks when they see you." The thought darkened his mood.

"You do and I'll have your housekeeper short-sheet your bed! Again, there should be perks to getting dressed like this, and getting laid should be one of them."

"I'll pretend I didn't hear that," he muttered and took another sip of his drink.

"You not only promised to come tonight, you swore you'd behave."

Ian scowled. "Good behavior ought to be optional considering the way he flaunts his assets," he said with a nod toward where Robert Dare held court.

Around him sat his second wife of nine years, Savannah Dare, and their daughter, Sienna, along with their nearest and dearest country club friends. Missing were their other two sons, but they'd show up soon.

Olivia placed a hand on his shoulder. "He loves her, you know. And Mom's made her peace."

"Mom had no choice once she found out about *her*."

Robert Dare had met the much younger Savannah Sheppard and, to hear him tell it, fallen instantly in love. She was now the mother of his three other children, the oldest of whom was twenty-five. Ian had just turned thirty. Anyone could do the math and come up with two families at the same time. The man was beyond fertile, that was for damned sure.

At the reminder, Ian finished his drink and placed the tumbler on a passing server's tray. "I showed my face. I'm out of here." He started for the exit.

"Ian, hold on," his sister said, frustration in her tone.

"What? Do you want me to wait until they sing 'Happy Birthday'? No thanks. I'm leaving."

Before they could continue the discussion, their half brother Alex strode through the double entrance with a spectacular-looking woman holding tightly to his arm, and Ian's plans changed.

Because of *her*.

Some people had presence; others merely wished they possessed that magic something. In her bold, red dress and fuck-me heels, she owned the room. And he wanted to own her. Petite and curvy, with long, chocolate-brown hair that fell down her back in wild curls, she was the antithesis of every too-thin female he'd dated and kept at arm's length. But she was with his half brother, which meant he had to steer clear.

"I thought you were leaving," Olivia said from beside him.

"I am." He should. If he could tear his gaze away from *her*.

"If you wait for Tyler and Scott, you might just relax enough to have fun," she said of their brothers. "Come on, please?" Olivia used the pleading tone he never could resist.

"Yeah, please, Ian? Come on," his sister Avery said, joining them, looking equally mature in a silver gown that showed way too much cleavage. At twenty-two, she was similar in coloring and looks to Olivia, and he wasn't any more ready to think of her as a grown-up—never mind letting other men ogle her—than he was with her sister.

Ian set his jaw, amazed these two hadn't been the death of him yet.

"So what am I begging him to do?" Avery asked Olivia.

Olivia grinned. "I want him to stay and hang out for a while. Having fun is probably out of the question, but I'm trying to persuade him to let loose."

"Brat," he muttered, unable to hold back a smile at Olivia's persistence.

He stole another glance at his lady in red. He could no more leave than he could approach her, he thought, frustrated because he was a man of action, and right now, he could do nothing but watch her.

"Well?" Olivia asked.

He forced his gaze to his sister and smiled. "Because you two asked so nicely, I'll stay." But his attention remained on the woman now dancing and laughing with his half brother.

*   *   *

Riley Taylor felt his eyes on her from the moment she entered the elegantly decorated ballroom on the arm of another man. As it was, her heels made it difficult enough to maneuver gracefully. Knowing a devastatingly sexy man watched her every move only made not falling on her ass even more of a challenge.

Alex Dare, her best friend, was oblivious. Being the star quarterback of the Tampa Breakers meant he was used to stares and attention. Riley wasn't. And since this was his father's birthday bash, he knew everyone here. She didn't.

She definitely didn't know *him*. She'd managed to avoid this annual party in the past with a legitimate work excuse one year, the flu another, but this year,

Alex knew she was down in the dumps due to job problems, and he'd insisted she come along and have a good time.

While Alex danced with his mother then sisters, she headed for the bar and asked the bartender for a glass of ice water. She took a sip and turned to go find a seat, someplace where she could get off her feet and slip free of her offending heels.

She'd barely taken half a step when she bumped into a hard, suit-clad body. The accompanying jolt sent her water spilling from the top of her glass and into her cleavage. The chill startled her as much as the liquid that dripped down her chest.

"Oh!" She teetered on her stilettos, and big, warm hands grasped her shoulders, steadying her.

She gathered herself and looked up into the face of the man she'd been covertly watching. "You," she said on a breathy whisper.

His eyes, a steely gray with a hint of blue in the depths, sparkled in amusement and something more. "Glad you noticed me too."

She blinked, mortified, no words rushing into her brain to save her. She was too busy taking him in. Dark brown hair stylishly cut, cheekbones perfectly carved, and a strong jaw completed the package. And the most intense heat emanated from his touch as he held on to her arms. His big hands made her feel small, not an easy feat when she was always conscious of her too-full curves.

She breathed in deeply and was treated to a masculine, woodsy scent that turned her insides to pure mush. Full-scale awareness rocked her to her core. This man hit all her right buttons.

"Are you all right?" he asked.

"I'm fine." Or she would be if he'd release her so she could think. Instead of telling him so, she continued to stare into his handsome face.

"You certainly are," he murmured.

A heated flush rushed to her cheeks at the compliment, and a delicious warmth invaded her system.

"I'm sorry about the spill," he said.

At least she hoped he was oblivious to her ridiculous attraction to him.

"You're wet." He released her and reached for a napkin from the bar.

Yes, she was. In wholly inappropriate ways considering they'd barely met. Desire pulsed through her veins. Oh my God, what was it about this man that caused reactions in her body another man would have to work overtime to achieve?

He pressed the thin paper napkin against her chest and neck. He didn't linger, didn't stroke her anywhere he shouldn't, but she could swear she felt the heat of his fingertips against her skin. Between his heady scent and his deliberate touch, her nerves felt raw and exposed. Her breasts swelled, her nipples peaked, and she shivered, her body tightening in places she'd long thought dormant. If he noticed, he was too much of a gentleman to say.

No man had ever awakened her senses this way before. Sometimes she wondered if that was a deliberate choice on her part. Obviously not, she thought and forced herself to step back, away from his potent aura.

He crinkled the napkin and placed the paper onto the bar.

"Thank you," she said.

"My pleasure." The word, laced with sexual innuendo, rolled off his tongue, and his eyes darkened to a deep indigo, an indication that this crazy attraction she experienced wasn't one-sided.

"Maybe now we can move on to introductions. I'm Ian Dare," he said.

She swallowed hard, disappointment rushing through her as she realized, for all her awareness of him, he was the one man at this party she ought to stay away from. "Alex's brother."

"Half brother," he bit out.

"Yes." She understood his pointed correction. Alex wouldn't want any more of a connection to Ian than Ian did to Alex.

"You have your father's eyes," she couldn't help

but note.

His expression changed, going from warm to cold in an instant. "I hope that's the only thing you think that bastard and I have in common."

Riley raised her eyebrows at the bitter tone. Okay, she understood he had his reasons, but she was a stranger.

Ian shrugged, his broad shoulders rolling beneath his tailored, dark suit. "What can I say? Only a bastard would live two separate lives with two separate families at the same time."

"You do lay it out there," she murmured.

His eyes glittered like silver ice. "It's not like everyone here doesn't know it."

Though she ought to change the subject, he'd been open, so she decided to ask what was on her mind. "If you're still so angry with him, why come for his birthday?"

"Because my sisters asked me to," he said, his tone turning warm and indulgent.

A hint of an easier expression changed his face from hard and unyielding to devastatingly sexy once more.

"Avery and Olivia are much more forgiving than me," he explained.

She smiled at his obvious affection for his siblings. As an only child, she envied them a caring, older brother. At least she'd had Alex, she thought and glanced around looking for the man who'd brought her here. She found him on the dance floor, still with his mother, and relaxed.

"Back to introductions," Ian said. "You know my name; now it's your turn."

"Riley Taylor."

"Alex's girlfriend," he said with disappointment. "I saw you two walk in."

That's what he thought? "No, we're friends. More like brother and sister than anything else."

His eyes lit up, and she caught a glimpse of yet another expression—pleasantly surprised. "That's the best news I've heard all night," he said in a deep, compelling tone, his hot gaze never leaving hers.

At a loss for words, Riley remained silent.

"So, Ms. Riley Taylor, where were you off to in such a hurry?" he asked.

"I wanted to rest my feet," she admitted.

He glanced down at her legs, taking in her red pumps. "Ahh. Well, I have just the place."

Before she could argue—and if she'd realized he'd planned to drag her off alone, she might have—Ian grasped her arm and guided her to the exit at the far side of the room.

"Ian—"

"Shh. You'll thank me later. I promise." He

pushed open the door, and they stepped out onto a deck that wasn't in use this evening.

Sticky, night air surrounded them, but being a Floridian, she was used to it, and obviously so was he. His arm still cupping her elbow, he led her to a small love seat and gestured for her to sit.

She sensed he was a man who often got his way, and though she'd never found that trait attractive before, on him, it worked. She settled into the soft cushions. He did the same, leaving no space between them, and she liked the feel of his hard body aligned with hers. Her heart beat hard in her chest, excitement and arousal pounding away inside her.

Around them, it was dark, the only light coming from sconces on the nearby building.

"Put your feet up." He pointed to the table in front of them.

"Bossy," she murmured.

Ian grinned. He was and was damned proud of it. "You're the one who said your feet hurt," he reminded her.

"True." She shot him a sheepish look that was nothing short of adorable.

The reverberation in her throat went straight to Ian's cock, and he shifted in his seat, pure sexual desire now pumping through his veins.

He'd been pissed off and bored at his father's ridiculous birthday gala. Even his sisters had barely been able to coax a smile from him. Then *she'd* walked into the room.

Because she was with his half brother, Ian hadn't planned on approaching her, but the minute he'd caught sight of her alone at the bar, he'd gone after her, compelled by a force beyond his understanding. Finding out she and Alex were just friends had made his night because she'd provide a perfect distraction to the pain that followed him whenever his father's other family was near.

"Shoes?" he reminded her.

She dipped her head and slipped off her heels, moaning in obvious relief.

"That sound makes me think of other things," he said, capturing her gaze.

"Such as?" She unconsciously swayed closer, and he suppressed a grin.

"Sex. With you."

"Oh." Her lips parted with the word, and Ian couldn't tear his gaze away from her lush, red-painted mouth.

A mouth he could envision many uses for, none of them tame.

"Is this how you charm all your women?" she asked. "Because I'm not sure it's working." A teasing smile lifted her lips, contradicting her words.

He had her, all right, as much as she had him.

He kept his gaze on her face, but he wasn't a complete gentleman and couldn't resist brushing his hand over her tight nipples showing through the fabric of her dress.

Her eyes widened in surprise at the same time a soft moan escaped, sealing her fate. He slid one arm across the love seat until his fingers hit her mass of curls, and he wrapped his hand in the thick strands. Then, tugging her close, he sealed his mouth over hers. She opened for him immediately. The first taste was a mere preview, not nearly enough, and he deepened the kiss, taking more.

Sweet, hot, and her tongue tangled with his. He gripped her hair harder, wanting still more. She was like all his favorite vices in one delectable package. Best of all, she kissed him back, every inch a willing, giving partner.

He was a man who dominated and took, but from the minute he tasted her, he gave as well. If his brain were clear, he'd have pulled back immediately, but she reached out and gripped his shoulders, curling her fingers through the fabric of his shirt, her nails digging into his skin. Each thrust of his tongue in her mouth mimicked what he really wanted, and his cock hardened even more.

"You've got to be kidding me," his half brother

said, interrupting at the worst possible moment.

He would have taken his time, but Riley jumped, pushing at his chest and backing away from him at the same time.

"Alex!"

"Yeah. The guy who brought you here, remember?"

Ian cursed his brother's interruption as much as he welcomed the reminder that this woman represented everything Ian resented. His half brother's friend. Alex, with whom he had a rivalry that would have done real siblings proud.

The oldest sibling in the *other* family was everything Ian wasn't. Brash, loud, tattoos on his forearms, and he threw a mean football as quarterback of the Tampa Breakers. Ian, meanwhile, was more of a thinker, president of the Breakers' rivals, the Miami Thunder, owned by his father's estranged brother, Ian's uncle.

Riley jumped up, smoothing her dress and rubbing at her swollen lips, doing nothing to ease the tension emanating from her best friend.

Ian took his time standing.

"I see you met my brother," Alex said, his tone tight.

Riley swallowed hard. "We were just—"

"Getting better acquainted," Ian said in a seductive tone meant to taunt Alex and imply just how much better he now knew Riley.

A muscle ticked in the other man's jaw. "Ready to go back inside?" Alex asked her.

Neither one of them would make a scene at this mockery of a family event.

"Yes." She didn't meet Ian's gaze as she walked around him and came up alongside Alex.

"Good because my dad's been asking for you. He said it's been too long since he's seen you," Alex said, taunting Ian back with the mention of the one person sure to piss him off.

Despite knowing better, Ian took the bait. "Go on. We were finished anyway," he said, dismissing Riley as surely as she'd done to him.

Never mind that she was obviously torn between her friend and whatever had just happened between them; she'd chosen Alex. A choice Ian had been through before and come out on the same wrong end.

In what appeared to be a deliberately possessive move, Alex wrapped an arm around her waist and led her back inside. Ian watched, ignoring the twisting pain in his gut at the sight. Which was ridiculous. He didn't have any emotional investment in Riley Taylor. He didn't do emotion, period. He viewed relationships through the lens of his father's adultery, finding it easier to remain on the outside looking in.

Distance was his friend. Sex worked for him. It

was love and commitment he distrusted. So no matter how different that brief moment with Riley had been, that was all it was.

A moment.

One that would never happen again.

*   *   *

Riley followed Alex onto the dance floor in silence. They hadn't spoken a word to each other since she'd let him lead her away from Ian. She understood his shocked reaction and wanted to soothe his frazzled nerves but didn't know how. Not when her own nerves were so raw from one simple kiss.

Except nothing about Ian was simple, and that kiss left her reeling. From the minute his lips touched hers, everything else around her had ceased to matter. The tug of arousal hit her in the pit of her stomach, in her scalp as his fingers tugged her hair, in the weight of her breasts, between her thighs and, most telling, in her mind. He was a strong man, the kind who knew what he wanted and who liked to get his way. The type of man she usually avoided and for good reason.

But she'd never experienced chemistry so strong before. His pull was so compelling she'd willingly followed him outside regardless of the fact that she knew without a doubt her closest friend in the world would be hurt if she got close to Ian.

"Are you going to talk to me?" Alex asked, breaking into her thoughts.

"I'm not sure what to say."

On the one hand, he didn't have a say in her personal life. She didn't owe him an apology. On the other, he was her everything. The child she'd grown up next door to and the best friend who'd saved her sanity and given her a safe haven from her abusive father.

She was wrong. She knew exactly what to say. "I'm sorry."

He touched his forehead to hers. "I don't know what came over me. I found you two kissing, and I saw red."

"It was just chemistry." She let out a shaky laugh, knowing that term was too benign for what had passed between her and Ian.

"I don't want you to get hurt. The man doesn't do relationships, Ri. He uses women and moves on."

"Umm, Pot/Kettle?" she asked him. Alex moved from woman to woman just as he'd accused his half brother of doing.

He'd even kissed *her* once. Horn dog that he was, he said he'd had to try, but they both agreed there was no spark and their friendship meant way too much to throw away for a quick tumble between the sheets.

Alex frowned. "Maybe so, but that doesn't change

the facts about him. I don't want you to get hurt."

"I won't," she assured him, even as her heart picked up speed when she caught sight of Ian watching them from across the room.

Drink in hand, brooding expression on his face, his stare never wavered.

She curled her hands into the suit fabric covering Alex's shoulders and assured herself she was telling the truth.

"What if he was using you to get to me?"

"Because the man can't be interested in me for me?" she asked, her pride wounded despite the fact that Alex was just trying to protect her.

Alex slowed his steps and leaned back to look into her eyes. "That's not what I meant, and you know it. Any man would be lucky to have you, and I'd never get between you and the right guy." A muscle pulsed in Alex's right temple, a sure sign of tension and stress. "But Ian's not that guy."

She swallowed hard, hating that he just might be right. Riley wasn't into one-night stands. Which was why her body's combustible reaction to Ian Dare confused and confounded her. How far would she have let him go if Alex hadn't interrupted? Much further than she'd like to imagine, and her body responded with a full-out shiver at the thought.

"Now can we forget about him?"

Not likely, she thought, when his gaze burned hotter than his kiss. Somehow she managed to swallow over the lump in her throat and give Alex the answer he sought. "Sure."

Pleased, Alex pulled her back into his arms to continue their slow dance. Around them, other guests, mostly his father's age, moved slowly in time to the music.

"Did I mention how much I appreciate you coming here with me?" Obviously trying to ease the tension between them, he shot her the same charming grin that had women thinking they were special.

Riley knew better. She *was* special to him, and if he ever turned his brand of protectiveness on the right kind of woman and not the groupies he preferred, he might find himself settled and happy one day. Sadly, he didn't seem to be on that path.

She decided to let their disagreement over Ian go. "I believe you've mentioned how wonderful I am a couple of times. But you still owe me one," Riley said. Parties like this weren't her thing.

"It took your mind off your job stress, right?" he asked.

She nodded. "Yes, and let's not even talk about that right now." Monday was soon enough to deal with her new boss.

"You got it. Ready for a break?" he asked.

She nodded. Unable to help herself, she glanced over where she'd seen Ian earlier, but he was gone. The disappointment twisting the pit of her stomach was disproportional to the amount of time she'd known him, and she blamed that kiss.

Her lips still tingled, and if she closed her eyes and ran her tongue over them, she could taste his heady, masculine flavor. Somehow she had to shake him from her thoughts. Alex's reaction to seeing them together meant Riley couldn't allow herself the luxury of indulging in anything more with Ian.

Not even in her thoughts or dreams.

About the Author

Carly Phillips is the *N.Y. Times* and *USA Today* Best-selling Author of over 50 sexy contemporary romance novels featuring hot men, strong women and the emotionally compelling stories her readers have come to expect and love. Carly's career spans over a decade and a half with various New York publishing houses, and she is now an Indie author who runs her own business and loves every exciting minute of her publishing journey. Carly is happily married to her college sweetheart, the mother of two nearly adult daughters and three crazy dogs (two wheaten terriers and one mutant Havanese) who star on her Facebook Fan Page and website. Carly loves social media and is always around to interact with her readers. You can find out more about Carly at www.carlyphillips.com.

CARLY'S BOOKLIST
by Series

Billionaire Bad Boys Reading Order:

Book 1: Going Down Easy

Book 2: Going Down Fast

Book 3: Going Down Hard

Dirty, Sexy Reading Order:

Book 1: Dirty Sexy Saint

Book 2: Dirty Sexy Inked

Book 3: Dirty Sexy Cuffed

Book 4: Dirty Sexy Sinner

Dare to Love Series Reading Order:

Book 1: Dare to Love (Ian & Riley)

Book 2: Dare to Desire (Alex & Madison)

Book 3: Dare to Touch (Olivia & Dylan)

Book 4: Dare to Hold (Scott & Meg)

Book 5: Dare to Rock (Avery & Grey)

Book 6: Dare to Take (Tyler & Ella)

*each book can stand alone for your reading enjoyment

DARE NY Series (NY Dare Cousins) Reading Order:

Book 1: Dare to Surrender (Gabe & Isabelle)

Book 2: Dare to Submit (Decklan & Amanda)

Book 3: Dare to Seduce (Max & Lucy)

*The NY books are more erotic/hotter books

Unexpected Love Series

The Right Choice

Suddenly Love

Perfect Partners

Unexpected Chances

Worthy of Love

Carly's Earlier Traditionally Published Books

Serendipity Series

Serendipity

Destiny

Karma

Serendipity's Finest Series

Perfect Fit

Perfect Fling

Perfect Together

Serendipity Novellas

Fated

Hot Summer Nights (Perfect Stranger)

Bachelor Blog Series

Kiss Me If You Can

Love Me If You Dare

Lucky Series

Lucky Charm

Lucky Streak

Lucky Break

Ty and Hunter Series

Cross My Heart

Sealed with a Kiss

Hot Zone Series

Hot Stuff

Hot Number

Hot Item

Hot Property

Costas Sisters Series

Summer Lovin'

Under the Boardwalk

Chandler Brothers Series

The Bachelor

The Playboy

The Heartbreaker

Stand Alone Titles

Brazen

Seduce Me

Secret Fantasy

54425726R00175

Made in the USA
Lexington, KY
15 August 2016